A
Cry in the Night

Allison

This Book Belongs to:

**Other Apple Paperbacks
you will enjoy:**

A Cry in the Night

Carol Ellis

AN
APPLE
PAPERBACK

SCHOLASTIC INC.
New York Toronto London Auckland Sydney

ISBN 0-590-42845-4

12 11 10 9 8 7 6 5 4 3 2 1   0 1 2 3 4 5/9

Printed in the U.S.A.   40
First Scholastic printing, February 1990

1

"Aren't we there yet?" Molly Bishop's little brother asked for the tenth time. "We've been in Massachusetts for an hour. When do we get to where we're going?"

Molly kept her eyes closed. She hadn't been asleep; she'd been pretending she was galloping along on a horse named Blackjack. Her bike was the best thing for the Blackjack daydream, but a car was good, too, because it went so fast.

Molly was twelve now, and she didn't pretend things like that as much as she used to. But on her bike or in a car, nobody needed to know. Besides, if she kept her eyes closed, everyone would think she was asleep and leave her alone.

"My back's all hot and sticky," Sam complained. "Can't we stop and get some Coke or something?"

"A Coke won't cool your back off," John Bishop said.

Molly could tell by their father's tone of voice that he wasn't going to stop the car for a Coke.

"I know, but when I get out to get it the air will," Sam said.

Molly wished Sam would give up. Arguing wasn't going to help. Their father was the most easygoing person in the world, except when he was driving on a highway.

"You're eight, Sam," Mr. Bishop reminded him. "I think that's old enough to travel in a car without having to stop every fifteen miles, don't you?"

"But my stomach feels real funny." Sam's voice was getting whiny. "Honest, Dad, a soda would help."

Molly heard her father take a breath, but before he could say anything, Katherine spoke up. "How about some Kool-Aid, Sam? There's still plenty in the thermos."

Molly immediately opened her eyes and sat up straight. "Kool-Aid won't work," she said. "It's not carbonated. He needs the fizz to make him burp."

There was a short silence. Then Mr. Bishop said, "Well. You're not asleep after all."

Molly met his eyes in the rearview mirror and felt herself blush. Why hadn't she kept her mouth shut? Now they thought she'd just been waiting to pounce on something Katherine said. And she hadn't, not this time, anyway. The words had just popped out. Glancing into the mirror again, she caught her father exchanging a *look* with Katherine. Katherine's look said, *There she goes again. Anything to disagree with me.* Her father's look said, *I know, I know. But we have to be patient.*

Molly had seen plenty of those looks since her father and Katherine had gotten married seven months ago. But she couldn't seem to help herself, not where Katherine was concerned. She didn't mean to be nasty to her; she didn't even argue with her. What she *tried* to do was ignore her. But then Katherine would do something stupid, like offering Kool-Aid for a shaky stomach, and Molly's mouth seemed to take on a mind of its own.

"Well, since you're not sleeping, maybe you can play a game with Sam, help take his mind off his stomach," Mr. Bishop said. "I think we can make Lynnton before dark if I don't stop."

"Okay." Molly would much rather have gone back to her daydream. But she'd given herself away by putting down the Kool-Aid suggestion, so she was stuck. She shouldn't really mind playing with Sam, she reminded herself. After all, somebody had to. Her father was driving, and Katherine had already buried her head in a folder of legal papers again.

If their mother had been here, she'd have known exactly what to do with Sam. She would have known better than to offer him Kool-Aid, too. The minute Sam started getting restless, she would have given him a sip of 7-Up, which she always brought on car trips, and then gotten him interested in counting out-of-state license plates or playing a word game.

But their mother wasn't here. Ellen Bishop had died three years ago from a weak blood vessel — an aneurysm — in her brain. The only clue that anything had been wrong was a few days of fierce headaches. She'd made an appointment to see the doctor, but she never got to keep it.

For weeks afterward, Molly would hear her mother's voice, calling her to dinner, asking her to find Sam, telling her to clean her room. Her father said that was normal, and that she'd stop hearing it after a while. He was right. Molly did stop hearing her mother's voice, but she'd never stopped missing it.

"Molly!" Sam was prodding her leg with the toe of his grungy sneaker. His gray eyes glittered behind his glasses and he'd already forgotten about his sticky back and queasy stomach. "Let's play 'Who Am I?' " he said. "I already thought of somebody; you'll never guess this one."

Molly shoved his foot away, but she smiled when she did it. Sam was okay, for a little brother. He used to drive her crazy when he was younger, always arguing with whatever anyone said. But he didn't do that so often anymore, and the two of them had gotten closer. Her father said it was because Sam had started to grow up, but Molly knew the real reason was because they'd both lost their mother.

"Come on, Molly, start!" Sam urged.

"Okay. Are you a boy?" Molly asked.

"Nope."

"Then you're a girl. Or a woman, right?"

"Wrong!" he hooted. "I told you you'd never guess it."

Molly pretended to think hard. She was pretty sure she already knew the answer: E.T. Sam had seen the movie two years ago at a friend's house and it was still his all-time favorite. He rented the video every chance he got.

"Then you must be a robot," Molly guessed, deliberately getting it wrong. "R2-D2."

"Nope! You're not even close!" Sam grinned and shoved himself back by pushing his feet hard against the front seat. This jounced Katherine, who slapped her hand over her papers to keep them from sliding out of her lap.

"Sorry," Sam murmured.

"Never mind." Katherine shuffled the papers and stuck them back in the folder. Then she turned around and smiled at him. "I'm ready for a break, anyway."

Molly didn't believe it. Katherine didn't seem to go anywhere without a folder of papers under her arm and a pencil in her hand. She'd even brought an electric typewriter on this trip.

Katherine Edelman was a lawyer. Not the kind you saw on television, who made dramatic pleas for innocent people. She almost never saw the inside of a courtroom. She spent her days writing contracts, making sure they were fair and legal and airtight. Molly's father said she was a good lawyer because she *didn't* have to go to court. Maybe so, Molly thought, but writing contracts sounded about as exciting as watching the grass grow.

Now, Katherine clicked open her brown leather briefcase — something else she never left home without — and stuck the folder inside. "So," she said to Sam, "how about if I play, too?"

"Sure." Sam pushed his glasses up on his nose and glanced at Molly. He knew how she felt about Katherine and he wanted to be sure this wouldn't make her mad. He got along better with their father's new wife than Molly did, but his first loyalty was to his sister. "Okay?" he asked.

"This is an open game," Mr. Bishop said from the driver's seat. "Anyone in the family is welcome to guess Sam's identity, right, Molly?"

"Right." Molly didn't care. She really didn't. Katherine could play all she wanted to. She still wouldn't belong.

Katherine didn't even look right, Molly thought. Everybody else in the family had sandy hair and either gray or hazel eyes. Katherine's eyes were dark brown, almost black, and so was her hair. The real Bishops were on the short side. Katherine was tall, with long legs that Molly often wished she could have.

And Katherine worked. Well, Ellen Bishop had worked, too, as a real estate agent. But she'd liked her free time as much as her job. Katherine seemed to think free time had been invented so she could get some extra work done. Even now, shooting questions at Sam, she looked like her mind was back in the brown leather briefcase.

"Not man, not woman, not robot," Katherine was saying crisply. "But I take it you're not human, either."

"Right," Sam agreed.

"Hmm." Katherine tapped her slender fingers against her mouth. "Are you a cartoon character?"

"Nope. Your turn, Mol," he said.

"A ghost?" Molly asked quickly, knowing it was wrong. Then she went back to thinking about Katherine.

When their father had first started dating her, a little over a year ago, Molly had almost been excited. It was like a book, or a TV romance. The two of them went out to dinner and to movies and parties. They met for lunch during the day, and talked on the phone at night if they weren't going out. Molly thought it was fun, until the day her father announced that he and Katherine were getting married. Molly didn't mind if her father dated. But marriage was something else. The three of them weren't even used to Ellen being gone. Then along came Katherine, with her answering machine and her legal papers, and everything had changed all over again.

"No, not Benji," Sam was saying. "You guys aren't even doing it right," he complained. "You have to ask what I look like and stuff. Come on, Molly."

"Okay." Molly decided Sam deserved a good game. "Are you in a movie?"

"Yes."

"Are you tall?"

"No. Katherine?"

Katherine shoved her pink-tinted sunglasses up on her head. "Do you walk on two legs?"

Sam nodded.

"Short, two legs, not human," Katherine murmured. "Oh," she said suddenly. "Are you from another planet?"

"Yes."

"Do you have a red spot on your chest?"

"Aww . . ."

"Are you E.T.?"

"Yes!" Sam flopped back against the seat, laughing. "How did you guess so fast?"

"I'm surprised I was so slow," Katherine said,

laughing, too. "You must have rented that video at least a dozen times."

"Okay, okay, I'll make the next one harder," Sam said. "Now it's your turn."

"All right, let's see." Katherine thought a minute. "Okay. Ready."

"We've got thirty miles, Sam," Mr. Bishop said. "I just saw the sign for Lynnton."

While Sam questioned Katherine, Molly stared out the window and thought about where they were going. The town of Lynnton, Massachusetts had been around since a group of Puritans had founded it in the late 1600s. Some of the old houses and shops were being restored now, so tourists could visit and get a feeling for what it was like living back then.

Molly's father was an accountant, and his company's newest client was the Lynnton Corporation. The company was sending him there to go over the books and help them get everything running smoothly. He knew it would take about a week, and since he had a vacation coming anyway, he'd decided to bring everybody along and give them all three weeks in Lynnton.

Molly knew she should be more excited than she was. Lynnton sounded like the perfect place for somebody who liked to pretend and imagine as much as she did. And she *was* looking forward to it. But her father kept calling this a "family

9

vacation," and every time he did, Molly remembered the last vacation they'd taken, when their mother was still alive.

They'd gone to Yellowstone Park, and they'd seen so many bears that when Molly heard a noise in their cabin one night, she'd had everybody convinced it was a huge bear. While Molly and Sam cowered in their sleeping bags, their parents had stumbled around with flashlights, grumbling and insisting that there was no way a bear could have gotten in. Finally their mother discovered a tiny mouse rummaging in a grocery sack. It had become a family joke, and even Sam still teased Molly about the grizzly mouse.

Now, Molly stared out at the rolling hills without really seeing them. Her throat ached and she had to keep swallowing hard until the lump of tears dissolved. This might be a vacation, but without her mother, it wasn't a *family* vacation.

"You're a lady in a movie, and you're not a cartoon," Sam said to Katherine. "And I've seen this movie, right?"

"Right."

"Okay." Sam pushed his glasses up again and stared at the roof of the car. He didn't pay that much attention to the "ladies" in movies. "Are there . . . um . . . spaceships in the movie?"

Katherine nodded.

"Oh, I know, I bet!" Sam started bouncing

10

around excitedly. "Do you wear a white dress?"

"Yes."

"And have funny-looking bunches of hair on the sides of your head?"

Katherine laughed. "I don't think they were supposed to be funny-looking, but yes."

"Princess Leia!" Sam shouted triumphantly.

"Right on target," Katherine said.

"And perfect timing," John Bishop added. "Fifteen more miles and we'll be in Lynnton. How's your stomach now, Sam?"

"Fine." Sam grinned and turned to Molly. "I didn't get any 'no' answers," he boasted. "I got 'em all right from beginning to end. You didn't have to ask a single one."

Molly grinned back at him. "That's okay," she said. "I would never have guessed it anyway."

Molly glanced at Katherine, who was already shuffling some more papers around. It was true, she thought. She would never have guessed it. Katherine was no Princess Leia.

2

It was seven o'clock but still light as the Bishops' car rounded its way down a hillside toward the town of Lynnton.

"It doesn't look so different to me," Sam remarked, staring out at the ordinary-looking houses and small stores. "I thought you said this place was real old."

"This is what they call New Lynnton. We haven't reached the old part yet," his father said. "Just wait."

In a few minutes, the road curved again and then narrowed and the ordinary-looking houses were left behind. Mr. Bishop stopped the car, and when Molly looked out the window to her right, she saw a long, packed-dirt road that had no sidewalks, no streetlights or parking meters, and no cars. On either side were clapboard houses with high-pitched roofs, built far apart. Some of the people walking along the road were obviously tourists. They wore shorts and T-shirts, and had cameras slung around their necks.

But among the tourists Molly saw women in long dresses of blue and green and dark red, with wide white collars and white caps that covered most of their hair. There were also men in coats with white collars, and capes, and wide-brimmed hats or knitted caps that looked a little like berets. Their pants came to just below their knees. They wore long thick stockings and leather shoes.

Even with the camera-carrying tourists, the old village of Lynnton looked like a piece of the past come to life.

"I thought the Puritan women only wore black or gray dresses," Molly said.

"Guess not," her father said. "They're trying to be very authentic here."

"Okay, this looks old," Sam said. "But it doesn't look very exciting."

"It's not a resort, Sam," Mr. Bishop told him. "It's a historical restoration. The Puritans didn't have ballfields and video hangouts."

"What's that thing?" Sam asked. He was pointing to a wooden structure at the end of the road, where there weren't any houses. It was long and thick, with round holes cut in it.

"The stocks," Katherine answered. "Ugly, isn't it?"

13

"Stocks, I know about those," Sam said. "The big hole's for the head and the little ones are for the hands." He squinted down the road at them, fascinated. "What did people do to get put in there?"

"Disobeyed the laws," Katherine said. "Things like being blasphemous — "

"What's that?"

"Swearing," Molly translated. "The Puritans were real religious."

Sam's eyes widened. "You mean you could get stuck in the stocks just for saying a curse word?"

"I think it was more for not believing in God, or at least not acting like you did," Mr. Bishop said. "I doubt if people walked around swearing a blue streak in those days. Anyway, I think they excommunicated people for not being religious enough."

"You're right," Katherine said. "The stocks were for other things, like drinking too much, or coming to the town and not having a job."

"That wasn't fair." Sam looked indignant.

"They did tend to be pretty strict with people who didn't behave the way they thought they should," his father agreed. "But some of their rules weren't so bad." His eyes twinkled. "Children, for instance, had plenty of chores — chopping wood, toting water — and if they didn't do

14

them . . . well, just be glad you're living in the twentieth century, Sam."

"Very funny, Dad."

Molly was still gazing out at the road. "Everybody looks like they're going to the same house," she said. "I wonder what's happening."

"Probably dinner," Mr. Bishop said. "An authentic candlelight meal and then back to the hotels and civilization. Old Lynnton closes down after dark — no electricity."

"What about our house?" Molly asked. "Does it have electricity?"

The Lynnton Corporation had found a house for the Bishops to stay in, one of the oldest in the town, dating back to the 1700s. Molly thought it would be romantic to try living without lights, at least for a while.

Sam obviously disagreed about the romance of no electricity. "It's gotta have it," he said. "How would we wash clothes?"

"You don't care about clean clothes," Molly teased. "You care about television."

"Dad?" Sam flopped halfway over the front seat, extremely concerned. "Are we gonna have electricity or not?"

Mr. Bishop chuckled and started the car. "Let's go see."

No cars were allowed in the old part of the

village, so they took the road that skirted it, eventually winding up at the other end of the town.

"This is the only house on this side of the village," Mr. Bishop said, "so I guess this must be it." He pulled the car to the side of the road and stopped.

The house was narrow, with a high, steep roof and well-weathered shingles. They could see the beginnings of the old village in the distance, what would have been about four blocks away. But on the other side of the house there was nothing but land — gently rolling and thick with trees.

"It's got lights," Sam said, pointing to the yellow glow of a bug light by the front door.

"It's also got visitors," Katherine commented. "Not Puritans, either. Look."

Parked in front of the house was a silver-gray Mercedes.

"Probably the welcoming committee," Mr. Bishop said. "Come on, let's go get welcomed."

Stiff and wrinkled from sitting in the car so long, the four of them climbed out and walked up to the wooden front door. Mr. Bishop had a key, but since someone was obviously inside, he decided to knock first. Just as he raised his hand, the door opened.

The two men stood just inside. One of them was tall and thin, with a long nose and bright blue eyes. His suit was the same color as the car, and looked just as expensive.

The second man was short and stout and rumpled-looking. "Mr. Bishop?" he said, holding out his hand. "I'm Bill Watkins of the Lynnton Corp. And this is Andrew Caleb; he's with the corporation, too, and he owns the house. His ancestors were some of the first Lynntonites. Well, come in, come in."

The Bishops stepped into a medium-sized room with a beamed ceiling and a wooden floor. A door at the side, and a narrow staircase and another door at the back led to other rooms, but this one was obviously the kitchen. There was a long wooden table in the middle and a huge open fireplace that took up most of one wall. Molly could imagine a big iron pot swinging over it, and a woman in a long white-collared dress stirring the fire.

Molly turned from this image just in time to hear Mr. Caleb, the tall, gray-suited man, say something about building a hotel on the land behind the house. "If we get the number of tourists we're hoping for, they'll need someplace to stay."

"Yes, indeed," Mr. Watkins said, rubbing his hands together. "And we want them to stay close by. More money for Lynnton that way."

Molly turned away and looked around some

17

more. It gave her a shiver to think that a Puritan family had actually lived here once, eaten in this same room, cooked food in that fireplace. Maybe they'd even had a girl her age, and a boy, like Sam, who hated to do chores.

Her mother would have loved this house, she knew. Ellen Bishop fell in love with every old house she'd sold. "They just breathe history," she used to say. "They have a past; you can feel it the minute you walk in."

"Well, we'll be going now," Mr. Caleb said, breaking into Molly's thoughts. "If you need anything, please just ask for it and we'll do our best to get it. And I'll stop by from time to time to make sure everything's all right."

The adults shook hands again, and then the two men left.

"Too bad the hotel's not built yet," John Bishop joked. "They told me this house was old, but they didn't say it was ancient."

Katherine laughed. "Come on, it's not so bad. Look, it's got a stove and a refrigerator."

But no dishwasher, Molly thought. And no microwave. She smiled to herself. Katherine did most of her cooking in the microwave. It would be interesting to see if she could boil water without one.

The room at the back was smaller than the kitchen, with a double bed, a dresser, and a pine chest taking up most of the space. At the end were two windows, looking out on a small, overgrown garden and then empty land.

Molly walked back to the kitchen and saw a door she hadn't noticed before, under the stairs. She pushed it open and discovered the bathroom. It was long and narrow, with no space to stand at the end where the stairs came down. At the other end was a tiny window, and in between were the basics: tub, toilet, and sink. The tub was a deep, old-fashioned one, with claw feet that someone had painted bright orange.

The room off the other side of the kitchen was furnished with a couch and chairs and tables. And a television, Molly saw. Sam would be relieved.

"I imagine this room was added on," her father said from behind her. "And there probably wasn't a wall between the kitchen and that back bedroom. I'd say it was one big kitchen-sitting room-bedroom. That's the way most of the houses were then."

He came and stood next to her, his hand on her shoulder. "According to Mr. Caleb, the upstairs was once a big sleeping loft. You got to it by a ladder. The stairway and walls were put up much later. There are two rooms up there; you and Sam can decide who gets which." He patted her shoulder. "They're going to be quite a bit smaller than you're used to."

"That's okay," Molly said quickly. "I love this place." She turned to him, ready to add, "Mother would have loved it, too." But then she saw Katherine striding toward them and she moved away. "Guess I'll go up and see my room," she said. "Then I'll come help bring the stuff in."

Sam was waiting for her at the top of the stairs. "It's really neat up here, Mol," he told her. "Except it's a good thing we're not any taller. The ceiling goes way down on one side."

Molly stepped up beside him onto a tiny landing just a few feet square. There was no hallway, just two doors opening off each side. She followed Sam into one of the rooms and saw that he'd already tossed his baseball glove and duffel bag on the bed.

"The rooms are just the same," he said, "except the other one has a mirror on the wall. I figured you'd want that."

"Yeah, but you're the one who needs it." Molly ducked out of the room just as his glove came sailing toward her head.

Sam was right — the room across the landing was the twin of his, with a window on the side and at the back, colorful rag rugs on the wood floor, a low bed, a chest of drawers, a chair, and a tall pine cupboard. Molly pulled open its doors and discovered that it was a free-standing closet.

The room was stuffy and hot. The back window

was painted shut, but she managed to get the side one open after a lot of pounding and flaking of paint. She had to kneel to do it, because the ceiling sloped so low that the bottom of the window was only six inches from the floor.

Molly sat there for a second, breathing in the warm August air that came through the ragged screen. It was dark outside now, and she could see flickering lights in the distance. The tourists must be having their candlelight dinner, she thought. Beyond that was a faint glow in the sky above the more modern part of Lynnton.

Turning around, Molly stood up and pulled the string on the bare, overhead light bulb. Then she studied her reflection in the mirror on the inside wall. Her yellow shorts, big striped T-shirt, and chin-length hair caught back in an orange plastic clip looked out of place in this house. Even the lights and the plumbing and the counters in the kitchen hadn't made the house let go of its past.

What would it have been like to live here? Molly wondered. What did almost-teenage girls do then, without bikes and television and jeans and phones?

Still staring in the mirror, Molly took the orange clip off and then piled her hair up on her head, trying to imagine what she'd look like in a white cap and a long dress. She turned off the light and moved around the room, feeling the imaginary swish of long skirts around her legs. All she could hear through the open window was the chirp of crickets, and it was easy to believe that the next sound she'd hear would be the creak of wagon wheels and the clop-clop of a horse's hooves.

Instead, what she heard next was a swoosh and gurgle of water, followed by what sounded like two huge metal pipes clanking against each other. When that faded, she heard the tinny musical introduction to a TV show, followed by Katherine calling her father's name.

Someone had used the bathroom, Sam had discovered the television, and Katherine was still in her life. Molly let go of her hair and headed for the door. Back to the present.

3

Two days later, Molly sat out in the overgrown backyard of the Caleb House, writing a letter to her best friend, Chris Buchanan. It was late afternoon, hot and still. Molly's sleeveless cotton top was plastered to her skin, and bugs kept crawling up her bare legs. Through the window, she could hear the television. Sam was trying to find a cartoon to watch. Her father was working at the office of the Lynnton Corporation, and Katherine was working in the downstairs bedroom, where she'd rigged up a desk using a wide board and cement blocks.

I thought the stocks were bad, Molly wrote. *But then yesterday we saw a demonstration of the ducking stool. Uggh! Sam thought it looked like fun. But it must have been awful. Imagine getting strapped to this seat and dunked under the water for not obeying your parents or something!!*

A ladybug landed on the notepad, and Molly

stopped writing until it explored the paper and then flew away.

Except for that stuff, though, I really like it here, she went on. *Our house is sort of all by itself, and I bought a pewter candlestick and put it in my room. It's neat. It has this great sloping ceiling, like an attic. Sometimes I pretend I actually lived back then.*

Chris wouldn't laugh at that, Molly knew. It hadn't been that long ago that they'd stopped playing with dolls.

I really don't think I would have liked it, though, she added. *Everybody minded everybody else's business. And when you got in trouble, the whole town knew about it!*

But some of the other things are fun. Yesterday I watched a man making shoes and another one weaving at an old-fashioned loom. Not everything is ready yet. There used to be a mill out by the river, but there's not much left of it. So they're going to rebuild it. Right now they take people out there in wagons for picnics. We're going tomorrow.

That is, we're going if you-know-who *can make it. She spends more time in the new part of Lynnton than the old part, because that's where the post office is. And when she's not mailing something, she's talking on the phone. To her office, of course. I don't know why she bothered to come.*

Chris was the only friend Molly could talk to about Katherine. Chris didn't say much, but at least she listened. That was the only bad part of this vacation — Molly couldn't gripe to Chris every time Katherine got on her nerves, which was at least ten times a day. Twice now she'd made Molly wait to make toast while she used her blow dryer. If they used too many appliances at once, all the fuses blew.

Molly's mother hadn't used a blow dryer. And even if she had, she would have let her kids have breakfast first. She would have *made* breakfast, too, or at least helped out. Especially on vacation. But Katherine wasn't hungry when she got up, so she didn't cook.

Thinking of food made Molly's stomach growl. She tucked her notepad under one arm and made her way through the tall weeds toward the side door that opened off the living room. Just as she reached it, Sam stepped out.

"I don't want to watch cartoons," he said. "Let's walk into town, okay?"

"Why don't you read a book?"

"I don't want to. I want to go into town."

Molly fanned the air in front of her face. "It's too hot."

"It is not. Come on, Molly, please?" He grinned

at her. "If you're so hot, maybe they'll let you go on the ducking stool."

"Very funny." Molly swiped at him with the pad of paper. "Okay," she said, changing her mind. "We can get come cider. Let's go."

"Um . . ." Sam didn't move. "Shouldn't we tell Katherine?"

"Yeah." Molly handed him her notebook. "Put this on my bed, okay? And don't read it. Then you can tell her on your way back out. I'll wait for you in front." Molly tried to say as little as possible to Katherine, even when it came to telling her they were going somewhere.

Two minutes later, Sam came out the front door carrying a small manila envelope. "She wants us to take this to the post office," he reported.

"Okay."

The two of them started along the road toward Old Lynnton.

"Mol?"

"What?"

"Do you hate Katherine?"

Molly looked at him. "I guess not," she said finally. "I just wish . . ." She shrugged and didn't finish.

"I know," Sam said. "You wish Mommy was still here."

Molly pulled a long weed out of the ground and

wrapped it around her finger. "Yeah."

Sam was walking backwards now, turning the envelope around and around in his hands. "Do you think Katherine hates us?"

Molly was pretty sure Katherine hated *her* sometimes. But Sam looked worried, so she didn't say so. "No. Why, what did she do?"

"Nothing." He tripped over a rock in the road and the envelope went skittering into the dust. He picked it up and wiped it off. "She's so polite. She never yells. Mommy used to yell sometimes, I remember."

Molly laughed. "You want to get yelled at?"

"Are you kidding?" He tried stuffing the envelope into his pocket, but it was a little too wide. "I don't think she understands kids much," he remarked.

"Well, that's *her* problem," Molly said. "Dad didn't exactly keep us a secret or anything. She knew we were around. Nobody made her marry him."

"Yeah, I know." Sam pushed his glasses up on his nose and smiled. "I guess Dad wouldn't let her stay if she hated us," he decided. "Maybe that's why she never yells, too."

That seemed to satisfy him, and he dashed off down the road. Molly followed more slowly. *She* wasn't satisfied at all. It was true, their father wouldn't have married Katherine if she hated his kids. And she didn't. Or at least she was smart enough not to show it.

What bothered Molly was that their father was really crazy about Katherine. He was always holding her hand, or putting his arm around her. They laughed a lot, too, especially when they were alone. Molly heard them at night, when she was lying upstairs in bed. And whenever he looked at her, his eyes sparkled.

It wasn't right, Molly thought. How could his eyes sparkle for Katherine? Didn't he remember Ellen anymore, and miss her? *Molly* hadn't forgotten. How could he?

"Hey, Molly, come on!" Sam was at the edge of the old village, waving the envelope like a banner. "There's somebody at the well."

Unwinding the weed from her finger, Molly dropped it in the road and hurried on. Four or five times a day, a man in knee-length pants and buckled shoes would haul buckets of water up, then take a big dipper and fill cups for the tourists. The water was cold and pure and better than cider on a hot day.

Molly got in line behind Sam and looked around while she waited for the man with the dipper. The tourists weren't the only ones lining up. The people in costume wanted some water, too, and she didn't blame them. Those outfits must have been baking hot.

Off to the side, Molly saw a girl about her age standing by herself. She was one of the "actors"; that's how Molly thought of the people in costume.

The girl's dress was faded blue, and its collar was limp, which was strange. All the other peoples' collars looked like they'd been starched and ironed. Her cap wasn't crisp and clean, either, and her blonde hair was tangled.

The strangest thing was that the people walking around the girl didn't even seem to notice her. And she wasn't paying any attention to them either. She wasn't paying attention to anything that Molly could see. She was just standing there, staring at nothing. At least, Molly thought she was staring. Her face wasn't really clear. Like her dress, everything about her seemed faded.

Maybe it was the sun, Molly thought. It was shimmering, like on a highway, and little ripples of heat made everything look wobbly.

But even though Molly couldn't see her clearly, something about the girl made Molly keep watching her. Her face reminded Molly of the time when she was about five and had wandered away from her mother in the grocery store. The girl looked lost, and ready to cry.

The man behind Molly tapped her on the shoulder. It was her turn. Molly held out a cup. Some of the water dripped onto her hands and she wiped them on her face to cool off.

When she looked back again, the girl was gone.

4

It was almost seven when Molly and Sam got back to the house. The car was already out front. Sam shouted for his father and ran to the door, both shoelaces flapping along the ground.

Molly followed him inside and stopped at the sink for a drink of water. She'd just shut the faucet off when she heard Sam's voice from the living room.

"Sorry," he muttered. "I forgot."

"How could you forget something you had in your hands?" Mr. Bishop sounded completely exasperated.

Molly wandered over to the doorway and looked in. Her father and Katherine were sitting together on the couch. Sam was standing in front of them, his back to Molly. Clutched in his hands was the manila envelope Katherine had given him to mail.

Molly had completely forgotten about it. They'd wandered around the village, drinking cider and

31

watching cloth being woven. Then they'd walked across to the modern part of town and hung around the book store. When they'd noticed it was getting late, they'd hurried back. Sam must have finally managed to wedge the envelope in his pocket, because Molly hadn't even seen it after a while.

"It was important, wasn't it?" Mr. Bishop asked Katherine. He looked tired and hot. And very grumpy.

Katherine nodded. "But there's nothing we can do now." She smiled, but Molly could tell she was annoyed.

"I guess I could take it now," Sam offered.

"No, it's time for dinner. Past time," his father told him. "You'll take it first thing in the morning." He looked up, noticed Molly, and frowned at her. "Why didn't you remind him?" he asked.

Molly shrugged. "I forgot, too," she said.

"And look at it." Mr. Bishop pointed to the envelope. It was creased and bent, sticky with cider, and smudged all over with dirty fingerprints.

"That's just the outside," Molly said. She was starting to get grumpy herself. "And it's not torn or anything, so I bet the very important papers inside are just fine."

"I don't like your tone of voice, Molly," her father said quickly. "Besides, that's not the point. The point is, you two have complete freedom all day to do almost anything you want, so when your mother asks — "

Molly felt her face go red. She didn't stop to think, she just shouted, "She's not my mother!"

"Molly — "

"And what's the big deal about a dumb letter?" Molly went on furiously. "What's going to happen if it gets there Friday instead of Thursday? Is her office going to go out of business or something?"

Mr. Bishop started to say something, but Katherine put her hand on his arm. "Never mind, John, please," she said. "Let's just forget it."

Molly had turned to leave, but now she whirled back around. "Then why didn't you say that in the first place?" she asked Katherine, her voice still loud. "If you're mad about the stupid letter, then be mad yourself! Don't make Dad do it!"

"Molly!" Mr. Bishop stood up. "That's enough! Apologize, now."

"I'm sorry!" Molly snapped, not meaning it. Then she turned and ran up to her room.

Dinner took forever. Molly's father insisted that she come down for it and do her usual chores like setting the table and making the salad. Then, while they ate, he was friendly and joking. He'd rigged up a shower in the claw-footed tub and taken one before dinner, so he was cool and comfortable again.

Molly could tell he felt bad about what had happened. This was his way of trying to make up. But he didn't feel half as bad as she did, and not because he'd chewed her out about the envelope, either.

He'd called Katherine "your mother." Had it just slipped out, from force of habit? Or did he really think of Katherine as their mother? He couldn't, he just couldn't.

"Molly?"

She looked up from her half-eaten slice of cold ham. Mr. Bishop was smiling at her.

"I was saying maybe we ought to drag out the Scrabble board and have a game," he told her. "Or how about Pictionary?"

"I vote for Scrabble!" Sam said. "I'm better at that."

"Fine with me," Mr. Bishop said.

"I'm lousy at both of them," Katherine laughed. "So it doesn't matter to me. Molly, which one do you vote for?"

"I'm kind of tired." Molly stood up. "I think I'll just take a shower and go to bed."

Later, Molly lay on her bed and listened to them playing Scrabble downstairs in the kitchen. She'd showered, put on shorty pajamas, and set the electric fan so that it blew straight at her. Above its soft whir, she could hear Sam's voice getting more and more excited.

"It is too a word!" he protested. "Alien's a word! Ask anybody!"

"We agree that it's a word, Sam," Mr. Bishop said. "But it's not spelled 'alian.' "

"Oh. Right."

It got quiet again and Molly turned onto her stomach so the fan could cool her back. She'd cried in the shower, and she felt like crying again now. She knew they all thought she was being a pain, even Sam. But she wasn't doing it on purpose. She just couldn't pretend that they were a happy family. Not tonight. She missed Ellen too much tonight.

She kept a picture of her mother on a small stool by her bed, and now she raised herself up and looked at it again. Ellen was standing in the kitchen, laughing because Molly had snuck up on her. It had been early in the morning, and her mother was in her old bathrobe and her hair was a mess. To Molly, she looked beautiful.

Molly flipped the pillow over to the cool side and angled her head so she could see the picture better. Her eyes filled and she closed them, the tears tickling as they slid across her nose.

She heard the voices murmuring downstairs, and then she must have dozed. When she opened her eyes again, her clock read midnight, and she could only hear her father and Katherine.

". . . never seem to be able to say or do the

35

right thing," Katherine was saying. "She's just determined not to give me a chance."

Molly was suddenly alert. She knew immediately who they were talking about. *She* was the subject of this late-night conversation. In the dark, she felt her face flush with anger and embarrassment.

"It's hard, I know," Mr. Bishop's voice was sympathetic. "I feel like I'm walking on eggs, too. Especially after what I said earlier. How long do you think I'll be in the doghouse for that?"

Molly knew he was talking about calling Katherine her mother.

"I'm sure it won't be for long. She loves you too much to hold a grudge."

Katherine said something else, but Molly couldn't make it out. She heard footsteps, and knew they were leaving the kitchen. Pretty soon she heard the pipes gurgle under the stairs, and water running. The old wood floor creaked a few more times, and then the house was silent.

It was ten after twelve. Molly lay there, wide awake. She hated both of them at that moment. How many times had they talked about her when they thought she couldn't hear? Lots, probably. Well, it was just too bad. She hadn't asked for things to be this way.

What if her father or Katherine lost a leg or went blind or something? Would they say, "Yes, it's terrible, but we just have to accept it?" She knew they wouldn't. Not for a long, long time. So how could they expect her to get used to not having Ellen? She never would. She'd always miss her.

Molly punched her pillow angrily. Why did they have to talk about her like this was all her fault? Like *she* was the problem? And why did they have to do it in the middle of the night? Now she'd never get back to sleep.

She turned over and breathed deeply. She heard the fan's whispery hum and listened to it closely. If she just concentrated on that, then maybe she could forget about everything else for a while.

Molly took more deep breaths. In and out, to the sound of the fan. She could feel herself starting to relax and she closed her eyes. It was working. Just a few more minutes, and . . .

"Mother!"

Molly's eyes snapped open. Had she dozed again? No, only a couple of minutes had gone by.

"Oh, Mother!"

The voice was soft and so sad that Molly's throat tightened. Was it Sam?

She sat up and put her feet on the floor, listening. Her door was open to catch any breeze that might blow through, and so was Sam's. She tiptoed out to the landing and peered into his room.

Sam was on his back, his mouth open, snoring gently. That must be what she'd heard, Molly thought. She padded back to her room. Before she reached the bed, she heard the voice again. Not Sam, she knew that for sure now. It was a girl's voice.

"Mother! Mother!"

Just the one word, over and over.

Molly's skin prickled, and she shivered in the heat. She shook her head and rubbed her bare arms. The voice was so close she kept expecting to feel its breath on her ear. But she was the only one breathing. She was the only one in the room. If it wasn't a dream, then what was it?

There was a deep sigh that seemed to fill the small room, and Molly felt her own chest rise and fall with it. The sigh came again, shorter and shorter, until the voice was sobbing.

Molly put her hands over her ears to shut it out. She was scared, but it was more than that. The sound was so sad, the voice was so filled with pain, that Molly couldn't stop her own tears. Her breathing became ragged and broken as she thought of her own mother. And then she was sobbing, too.

The voice cried out again, and this time Molly cried with it, "Mother!"

5

Molly? Molly, wake up!"
She heard her father's voice, and then the
overhead light was switched on. Mr. Bishop put
his arm around her shoulders and gave her a
gentle shake. "It's okay, honey. You were having
a dream."

Molly looked around, blinking in the harsh light.
Katherine stood in the doorway wrapped in a thin
cotton robe. Her father was in his summer sleep
outfit — old running shorts and a ragged T-shirt.
Both of them looked worried.

She wiped her cheeks and shook her head. "It
wasn't a dream."

"What's going on?" Sam was at the door, yawning widely.

"Molly had a dream," Mr. Bishop told him.
"Everything's fine, Sam; go on back to bed before
you wake up all the way."

Sam nodded and stumbled off, his eyes already
drifting closed.

"It wasn't a dream," Molly said again.

"We heard you call, Molly," Katherine said from the doorway.

" 'Mother,' right?" Molly asked. "You heard me call 'Mother.' "

Katherine nodded and looked at the floor.

"How many times?"

"What?"

"How many times did I say it?" Molly asked.

"Once," Katherine said, frowning. "But it was so loud, and we weren't asleep. . . ."

"Neither was I," Molly told her. "I heard it, too, only more than once, that's why I . . ."

Molly's father squeezed her shoulder. "I don't think you're really awake even yet," he said. He pulled her gently toward the bed. "Come on, see if you can get back to sleep."

Molly saw him look at Katherine and motion with his head. Katherine cleared her throat and smoothed back her hair. "I think I'll just go on downstairs," she said. "See you in the morning, Molly."

"See you." Molly sat down on the bed and her father sat next to her.

"I guess I know what caused this," he said. "You've been missing your mother; I had a bad day and took it out on you and Sam. And then I goofed and called Katherine your . . . well, you know." He rubbed his eyes and the back of his

40

neck. "It really was just a goof, Molly. I know you don't think of her as your mother and I don't expect you to."

Molly nodded.

"I wish you could try to think of her as part of the family, though," he said. "She's my wife and I love her. It would mean a lot if you could accept that."

Molly shifted around, but didn't say anything. Did he expect her to say, "Oh, okay, Dad," just like that? She couldn't.

Mr. Bishop stood up. "And I haven't forgotten your mother, in case that's something else you were worrying about. I'll never forget her, okay?"

"Okay." Molly stood up and hugged him. "I think I can sleep now."

"I'm not sure you ever stopped," he chuckled. "Good night, Molly."

"Night."

Molly waited while he turned off the light, then listened to his rubber flip-flops slapping down the stairs. When everything was quiet again, she lay down in bed. She knew she should think about what her father had said. But at the moment, she had something else on her mind.

It hadn't been a dream, she knew that. But she'd finally gone along with her father because she didn't feel like arguing. What was the point? He'd only heard *her* voice.

But she'd heard someone else's. She didn't know whose, or why. But until three in the morning when she finally fell asleep, she listened, wondering if she'd hear the voice again.

It rained sometime before sunrise, but by the time Molly went downstairs for breakfast, a strong breeze had driven the clouds away. The sky was a brilliant blue, and everything was crisp and sparkling. The mournful voice she'd heard in the dark, hot room didn't belong in such a beautiful day. But Molly could still hear it in her mind.

Sam had already left for the post office when Molly came down, so only her father and Katherine were in the kitchen.

"Well, well!" Mr. Bishop said in a hearty voice. "We thought you'd sleep in this morning."

Molly shook her head, yawning. "The bathroom pipes are like an alarm clock." She got a bowl and the Cheerios and took them to the table. As she poured the cereal into the dish, she looked up. Both of them were watching her.

Her father smiled brightly. "No more dreams?"

Oh, no, he was still worried, Molly thought. She hadn't heard the voice again, but if she kept insisting it wasn't a dream, he'd get even more worried. He might even suggest she talk to someone, like a psychiatrist.

"No dreams," she said, spooning up Cheerios.

Which was the truth. She smiled brightly, too, even at Katherine.

"Well, that's good!" Mr. Bishop finished his coffee and stood up. He picked up his briefcase, came around the table, and gave Molly a kiss. "See you later. Have fun at the picnic."

Molly had forgotten about it. But an hour later, as she and Sam and Katherine climbed onto the horse-drawn wagon that would take them to it, she was glad to be going. Maybe the picnic would make her forget that haunting voice.

There were six wagons, two for the "actors," and the rest for the tourists. The ride was bumpy, but Molly loved it. Clattering along a winding dirt road behind a team of gleaming brown horses made it easy to pretend she was living in the past.

After about fifteen minutes, they reached the creek. A little way beyond it was a small wooden house. The women in long dresses climbed down from the wagons and carried baskets and bundles inside.

The gristmill was close to the creek. Or what was left of the mill. To Molly it looked, at first, like a pile of rocks and a bunch of rotted boards. The tourists gathered around, and one of the men explained how it would look when it was rebuilt. Molly gradually understood that it was a sort of windmill, and she was able to imagine it standing there with its big fans open to catch the breeze.

While the tourists walked around, hearing about how the mill worked and about the Indian corn, wheat, and barley that once was grown nearby, the women actors were working in and around the small house. Wonderful smells began to drift through the air. People forgot about the mill and started thinking about food.

"What do you think, Sam?" Katherine asked as everybody moved toward the trestle tables that had been set up and piled with food.

Sam looked at the platters and bowls of corn-bread, beans, beef, and greens. "I'd rather have a hamburger," he said, reaching for a cup of cider.

Katherine laughed and put her arm around his shoulder. "To tell you the truth, I'm not that hungry, either. But I guess if I'd been working at a gristmill or out in the fields, I'd be ready for a big meal."

"Yeah, I guess so," Sam agreed. "A Big Mac, maybe."

Laughing together, the two of them took plates and moved down the table. Molly followed, listening to them talk and joke. Katherine had practically ignored her all morning. Oh, she talked to her, but just the basic stuff, like "How are you?" and "Are you ready to go?" She didn't try to start up any conversations.

Maybe this was Katherine's new way of dealing with her — as little as possible. It was fine with

Molly. But she wished her father could have come with them. With Sam and Katherine chatting away like good buddies, Molly felt like a third wheel. And no matter how nice the day was, or how much fun the picnic, nothing could shut out the memory of that voice.

Who was it? Why had she heard it? How could she have heard it when no one else had? Those were some of the questions Molly kept asking herself as she munched the warm cornbread and drank the cider.

She'd been scared when it happened, but the girl's voice itself wasn't frightening. Her sadness was what Molly remembered most. As if the girl were lost, or her mother was. Molly felt lost, too, lots of times, especially since Ellen had died and Katherine had come into their lives. Molly didn't understand what had happened the night before, but she knew there was nothing to be afraid of. How could she be scared of such a heartbroken voice?

After the meal, the tourists climbed back on the wagons for the drive back to Lynnton. The actors stayed behind to clean up and get ready for another bunch of tourists.

"Who's for ice cream?" Katherine asked when they got back to the village.

"Coke!" Sam voted. He drank it every chance he got. "I'm sick of cider."

"Molly?" Katherine said politely.

Molly was determined to be just as polite. "Fine with me," she said.

For soda, they had to walk to the deli in the new part of Lynnton. As they were leaving it, they saw Andrew Caleb driving by in his silvery car. He gave them a friendly wave.

"Just think," Katherine said. "We may be the very last people to stay in the old Caleb house."

"Why?" Sam asked.

"Well, because of the hotel," she told him. "People will stay there."

They walked along for a few more minutes, and then Katherine said, "Maybe I'll paint a picture of the house."

Sam looked up at her through his smudged glasses. "I didn't know you were a painter." He sounded impressed.

"I'm not," Katherine laughed. "But I think I could do a decent picture of the house if I try hard enough." They were getting near the house now, and she stopped and looked at it. "The hotel's not going to be glitzy or anything. Mr. Caleb was telling your father that they'll try for an old, understated look, sort of like an inn. I hope the house won't be overshadowed by it."

It was the first smart thing Molly had heard Katherine say.

*   *   *

46

That night, Molly heard the voice again. She kept quiet this time, even though it made her feel like crying. She lay in bed, listening to the girl calling for her mother, and wondered what terrible thing had happened to make her sound so sad.

"Mother?" The voice was dry, as if the girl had cried until her throat was raw. "Mother. Come back. You must. You must come back."

How many times had Molly said that herself? Hundreds, she guessed. Asking for something she knew was impossible. But asking anyway. No wonder she wasn't afraid. She and the girl had both lost their mothers. They were connected, somehow.

The voice only lasted a minute or so, and then it faded away. Before it did, Molly whispered, "I hear you. I know how you feel."

6

The worst part was keeping the voice a secret. Molly couldn't tell her father. She knew he'd have a long discussion with her about how important it was not to keep her feelings bottled up. He'd think she imagined the voice, and that it was really *Molly*, calling for Ellen. And that if she'd just accept the fact that Ellen was dead, the voice would stop.

Molly *knew* her mother was dead. That wasn't the problem. The problem was, she wanted Ellen back.

She couldn't talk to Katherine about the voice, naturally. She'd tried writing about it to Chris. But every time she put it down on paper, it seemed ridiculous, and she'd torn up the letters.

"Mol?" Sam was at the door of her room, looking impatient. "You said you'd be ready to go in five minutes. It's been twenty, already."

"Sorry." Molly slid from her bed and shut off the fan. "I was thinking. Let's go."

They were going into the village, as usual. There really wasn't much else to do. Molly didn't mind. Sam was already getting tired of the old town, but she loved it. She was glad she hadn't lived then, but it was fun to go there and pretend, just for a while.

As they let themselves out the front door, they saw Katherine. She'd bought an easel and some paints in a nearby town, and for two mornings now, she'd set them up across the road and worked on her painting.

Sam ran over to see, and Molly couldn't help following. She was curious to see if Katherine really could paint. Stepping behind Sam, she looked over Katherine's shoulder. Not much, so far. Just a sort of gray-brown blob that vaguely resembled a house.

"Is that *it?*" Sam asked. He didn't sound impressed anymore.

"It's an attempt," Katherine told him. "I've done about ten of them and they're all wrong."

"Maybe you should just take a picture of it," Sam suggested.

"I might have to." Katherine smiled and wiped her hands on her jeans. Molly had never seen her look so sloppy. "But I think I'll give it a few more tries before I give up. Are you two going into the village?"

Molly nodded.

Katherine picked up her brush and dabbed it in some reddish-brown paint. "See you later."

Molly nodded again and walked off with Sam.

"Gosh, she didn't even ask when we'd be back," Sam remarked. "She usually does. Do you think she's mad?"

Molly shook her head. "Not at you."

"I meant *you*, anyway," Sam said. He picked up a twig and started breaking it into small pieces. "She's always pretty nice to me, even after I messed up her envelope. And she was fun at the picnic. But after that night, when you yelled at her, she's been acting kind of weird with you."

"Tell me about it," Molly laughed. Sam looked worried, though, so Molly decided she'd better say something more. "She's just leaving me alone most of the time, that's all. She's not being weird; she's being polite, like you said."

"Yeah." He tossed the pieces of twig up into the air and tried to catch them. "You're acting weird, too, though."

"Me? What do you mean?"

"Like, you're not making any snotty remarks anymore."

"That's because of Dad," Molly explained. "It gets him really upset when I'm not nice to Katherine, so I decided I'd just act polite, too. See?"

"I guess," Sam said. "But it sure is a weird

50

family." He tossed the last piece of twig down and started to run. "Come on, let's go see if anybody's in the stocks!"

Sam was still fascinated with the stocks. He'd had his picture taken in them three times already. Most of the visitors did. That morning Molly left him there with a small group of tourists and wandered over to the meeting house. She hadn't visited it yet, because she didn't want to do everything in the first one or two days and then be left with nothing to see.

The Puritans didn't call it a church, she knew, because they used it for town meetings, too. It was a large square building with a belfry and leaded-glass windows, and it stood at the end of the road, a little bit away from the other houses. It didn't have a cross, and the windows weren't stained glass. It was very simple. To Molly it looked like an old-fashioned schoolhouse.

Inside was a large, bare room, with backless benches on either side of a center aisle. There wasn't a pulpit at the front, just a big wooden table. The bell rope hung right down into the middle of the aisle. Molly sat down on one of the benches and picked up a leaflet that explained what the Sabbath had been like back in the 1700s.

Everybody was expected to come to the services, it said. If they didn't, and failed to have a good excuse, they could be fined or punished. The stocks, again, Molly thought.

Women sat on one side of the aisle; men on the other. Molly looked around and wondered which side she was on.

Services lasted all day, with a break at noon, when people went home for dinner. Molly tried to imagine sitting on this hard bench for hours, listening to a sermon. She wasn't sure she could have done it. She knew Sam couldn't have.

Still, she enjoyed sitting here now, as long as she knew she could get up when she wanted to. Windows on both sides let a breeze blow through, and the air was almost cool inside. Maybe they hadn't called it a church, but it felt like one. The other people must have thought so, too, because they were talking in whispers.

Molly closed her eyes for a moment, listening to the quiet talk and feeling the soft breezes. Sam was funny, she thought, talking about what a weird family they were. He didn't miss much, even if he was only eight.

Someone coughed, then a little kid started whining that he was bored. Molly opened her eyes a little. Then she opened them wider.

There, at the end of the aisle where the minister would have stood, was the girl Molly had seen a couple of days before. Or thought she'd seen. She wore the same faded dress and her hair was still tangled. She didn't seem to notice anyone. And the people walking by and around her didn't seem to notice her.

As Molly watched, the girl slowly made her way up the aisle toward the door. When she was almost to Molly's bench, Molly stood up. She didn't know what she was going to say or do. Ask what was wrong, maybe, or ask if she could help. She had to do something, though. Someone had to help.

The girl was even with Molly's bench now. Molly cleared her throat and reached out with her hand. But the girl kept moving, staring straight ahead, as if Molly wasn't even there. As she passed, Molly heard a sigh. The sigh seemed to come from the very bottom of the girl's heart, and Molly could almost feel it within herself.

Still clutching the leaflet, Molly walked outside into the bright sunlight. The girl had walked a short distance from the meeting house, and now she had turned around to face it.

Molly glanced quickly around at the other people outside. They walked by the girl as if she didn't even exist. When she looked back at the girl, she felt her throat tighten with tears. The girl's hands were twisting the folds of her dress, and her eyes had the saddest look Molly had ever seen. She looked completely alone, and lost.

Molly took a step toward her. Someone had to do something. How could everyone ignore someone who was so unhappy?

And then Molly saw Sam. He was running toward her, his thick glasses glinting in the sun. He was behind the girl, running right at her.

"Sam, watch where you're going!"

Sam looked around, but he didn't see anyone in his way and he kept running.

"Sam, you're going to run right into her!"

"What?"

"I said, look out, you're — " But by then, Sam had reached Molly. He was standing by her side, breathing hard and laughing.

"What are you talking about?" he asked. "Run into who?"

Molly looked past him, but the girl was gone. Sam hadn't seen her. No one else had, either. No one but Molly had seen her.

"Molly?"

That's when Molly knew. The girl was there, but only for *her*. Just like the voice. She wanted Molly to see her. She wasn't real to anyone else. But somehow, for some reason, she was real to Molly.

7

M olly?" Sam said again.

Molly dragged her gaze away from the place where the girl had been and looked at Sam.

"Mol? What's going on?" He scratched his head and squinted up at her. "Are you trying to play a joke on me or something?"

Slowly Molly shook her head.

"Then what?" he asked. "You're acting really weird, Mol, you know?"

Molly smiled and shook her head again. "I'm *feeling* really weird. But it's no joke."

Sam shifted impatiently and sighed. "Then what?" he asked again. "Come on, Molly!"

Molly knew she had to tell somebody. This was just too amazing to keep to herself. "Okay, Sam. Let's head back to the house and I'll tell you."

On their second day in Lynnton, they'd found a path that veered off the road just past their house. It twisted its way into the town, ending just behind the meeting house. They'd never seen anybody else on it. It was shady and private, and that's where Molly told Sam about the voice, and the girl she'd seen. Hearing herself tell it, she knew how incredible it sounded. Incredible or not, though, it was true. She'd heard and seen a ghost. And she was the only one who had. For some reason, this ghost-girl had picked Molly to come to.

When she finished, Sam scuffed the toe of his sneaker in the dirt. Then he pulled a leaf off a tree and started shredding it. Finally he said, "I don't get it."

"I don't, either," Molly admitted.

He gave her a sideways look. "Are you scared?"

"I'm confused, I guess," Molly said. "But I'm not scared."

That was all Sam needed to hear. "Me, neither," he announced. "Man, a *ghost*! I don't believe it!" He took a flying leap along the path. "What are you going to do, Mol?" he yelled back over his shoulder.

That was a good question, Molly thought. What *was* she going to do? How did you communicate with a ghost or a spirit or whatever it was?

"I guess I'll try to find out who she is," she said. "And what she wants."

"How are you going to do that?"

"I don't know yet," Molly said. "But listen, Sam.

You've got to keep your mouth shut about it, okay?"

"You mean you're not telling Dad?"

"I'm not telling anybody, at least not until I know more." Molly stopped and put her hands on her hips. "And you can't tell, either, Sam. You promise?"

"I promise, I promise." Sam looked insulted. "I can keep a secret, you know." Then he took another flying leap and shouted, "Nobody would believe it, anyway!"

You're telling me, Molly thought.

The voice came again that night, when Molly was lying in bed. For a minute, she thought about getting Sam. But she knew he wouldn't be able to hear it. It was just for her.

"Mother, oh, Mother! Oh, no!"

Molly sat on the edge of her bed and listened. If only she could talk to her, ask her questions. But spirits didn't work like that, she guessed.

Why me? she wondered. And then, listening to the sorrowful voice, she knew. It was so simple, she didn't know why she hadn't thought of it before. The single word, Mother.

Molly's mother had died, and Molly had brought all her memories and pain into this room.

And the girl's mother? Well, of course, she'd

died. But how? Some awful sickness that they couldn't cure back then? Or maybe an accident — something horrible and careless that shouldn't have happened. That might explain why the girl's spirit couldn't rest.

But how could she find out what had happened? It was so many years ago. Where could she even start?

The voice grew louder and then broke into sobs. "Must I leave?" it cried. "Where shall I go? Oh, Mother, where shall I go?"

Molly's eyes widened. She couldn't see anything, but she could almost feel the crying. It was coming from the other end of the room, by the little window that her father had finally pried open.

The girl had lived here. Molly remembered her father saying that this used to be just a loft, a sleeping loft. Maybe this had been the girl's home, and after whatever had happened to her mother, she'd climbed up to this loft and cried.

The house was the place to start, Molly thought. If she could find out about the history of this house, she might find out what happened to the girl and her mother.

As Molly closed her eyes and thought about how to do it, the sobbing gradually faded until the room was quiet again. It was almost as if the spirit had been waiting for Molly to figure out what she had to do. And now that she had, it could stop crying and wait for her help.

"What do we know about this house?" Molly asked at breakfast the next morning.

"We know it's old." Mr. Bishop buttered a corn muffin. "And that its plumbing stinks."

"I don't mean the plumbing," Molly said. "I mean way before it even had plumbing. Who were the first people to live here?"

"Puritans, who else?" Sam said, reaching for the milk. "Anyway, who cares?"

Molly caught his eye and gave him what she hoped was a "knowing" look.

"Oh!" he said. He ducked his head and started eating his corn flakes.

"Oh, what?" his father asked.

Molly was trying to think of an answer when she was saved by a knock at the door. Katherine opened it, and everybody turned to see Andrew Caleb standing outside.

"Good morning," he said, stepping in. "I'm sorry to disturb you, but I wanted to check in and see how you're getting along. Everything's fine, I hope."

"Oh, yes, just fine," Mr. Bishop said. "We're very comfortable, thanks."

"Good, good," Mr. Caleb said. "I also wanted to let you know that there'll be a team of surveyors

59

out here sometime today." He glanced around the room and gave them all a smile. "They won't be any bother, I'm sure, but I thought you should know."

"Fine," Mr. Bishop said. "Thanks for telling us."

Mr. Caleb nodded. "Well, I'll be off."

"Wait!" Molly stood up and walked over to the door. "I mean, please. I wonder if I could ask you some questions."

"Oh, that's right," her father said. "Molly's taken a sudden interest in your house," he added to Mr. Caleb.

Andrew Caleb looked down at Molly and smiled. "What can I tell you?"

"I just wondered how old it is," she said. "And did your family always own it? I mean, were the Calebs the people who built it?"

"I'm afraid I know very little about its history," Mr. Caleb admitted. "I believe it was built in the mid-1700s and, as far as I know, the Calebs built it." He smiled again. "If this is a history project, one of the houses in the village might be better for it."

The history project was a good idea; Molly was glad he'd said it. It *was* sort of a history project, anyway. It just wasn't for school. "I guess so," she agreed. "But since we're staying in this house, this is the one I want to do."

"Then I'm afraid I can't be much help," Mr. Caleb told her. "I don't think the records have been kept up. It's not a very good example of the time, anyway. It's been added on to and modernized so that it's hardly recognizable. That's why I suggested one of the village houses. But I'll certainly give it some thought and see if I can remember anything."

"I just had an idea, Molly," Katherine said. "There must be a department of records or some place like it in Lynnton. You might be able to learn something there." She looked at Mr. Caleb. "Don't you think so?"

"I'm not sure their records go back that far," he said doubtfully.

"I think I'll check it out," Molly said. It was a good idea, even if it had come from Katherine.

"Well, I'll try to see if I can remember anything about the house, too." He glanced around the room again, nodding and smiling. "I have to be going. I'm glad you're getting along all right." He stepped outside and pulled the door shut behind him. In a moment, they heard his car take off down the road.

Katherine was right. The new part of Lynnton did have a Department of Records and Deeds. It was in the City Hall, along with the mayor's office and the water department and lots of other offices.

That afternoon, Molly walked into the records department with a spiral notebook in her hand and a pen in the pocket of her jean skirt, and looked around nervously. She'd done a few research papers in school, but she'd never done anything like this. She wasn't even sure what questions to ask.

But Molly knew she had to find out. She felt she'd made a promise that she couldn't break.

There was a long counter in the room. Behind it were desks and doors that led to other offices, Molly guessed. She walked to the counter and cleared her throat.

The woman at the desk looked up and smiled. "Can I help you?"

"I hope so," Molly said. "I need . . . I'm trying to find out about a certain house. It's here in Lynnton; my family's staying in it. It's on Selden Road and Mr. Andrew Caleb is the owner."

The woman nodded as if she was familiar with it. "What do you need to know about it?"

Molly opened her notebook, where she'd made a list. "Umm . . . when it was first built, and who lived in it."

"Who lived in it when?" the woman asked.

"Well . . . since it was built, I guess," Molly said. "I want to find out about the people."

"I'm not sure . . . hold on." The woman left her desk and went through one of the doors at the back. Molly thought all the records must be back there. Hopefully, she took the pen out of her pocket.

In a few minutes, the woman was back, shaking her head. "I'm afraid our records don't go back that far. The earliest date I found was in 1870, and I know the house is older than that."

"Mr. Caleb said he thought it was built in the 1700s," Molly said.

"At least!" The woman laughed. "As far as I know, it was always owned by Calebs. But our records aren't going to tell you much about the people who lived in it, anyway. We keep records of taxes and debts and variances . . . which are documents giving permission to make changes in the house," she explained.

"Well. Thank you." Molly slipped the pen back.

"But you know who might know something?" the woman asked. "George Bradbury. He's in charge of the museum."

"I didn't know there was one," Molly said.

"Well, it's not really open yet," the woman told her. "Lynnton's old, but this whole restoration thing is new. They spent most of their time and money getting the village ready. It'll be a little while before the museum's in shape."

"Where is it?" Molly asked.

"It's just down the road, right at the end, before you get into the old village." She frowned and lowered her voice. "George isn't the friendliest person in the world, I'm afraid. But he knows his history. If you don't rub him the wrong way, he just might help you out."

Her hopes up again, Molly thanked the woman and left City Hall. Just as she got outside, a silver-gray Mercedes pulled up and Andrew Caleb stepped out.

"Well . . . Molly, isn't it?" he said.

"Yes, hi, Mr. Caleb."

"And how's your search into the history of my house going?"

"Not too well," Molly admitted. "Yet."

He raised an eyebrow. " 'Yet'? Does that mean you have a lead?"

"I'm not sure." Molly told him about the museum and Mr. Bradbury. "I'm going there now."

"Yes, of course. George," he said. "I don't know why I didn't think of him myself."

"Well, the woman at the records department told me he wasn't very friendly," Molly said, "but I think I'll give him a try anyway."

"Of course. Let me know how it turns out." He nodded and walked off.

Molly watched after him for a moment, smiling to herself. He thought the house had been modernized too much to make a good "history" project. But what if she told him the house was haunted? She bet he'd change his mind!

8

From his long nose and skinny neck to the tips of his incredibly large feet, George Bradbury reminded Molly of Ichabod Crane. She half expected him to talk about the Headless Horseman, but what he said was, "Sorry, little girl. You've got the wrong place."

Molly decided to ignore the little girl bit. After all, she wanted his help. "Isn't this the Lynnton Museum?"

He peered down at her with small dark eyes. "Yes. Such as it is."

Molly smiled. "Then I've got the right place." She glanced around. It wasn't what she'd expected. They were in a small, dark hall with a door on each side and a narrow staircase at the back. The hall was filled with boxes and smelled musty. One of the doors opened onto a large room, and Molly could see tables with old iron tools and wooden things on them. In the other room, she could see part of an incredibly messy desk.

Mr. Bradbury looked at her as if she were an annoying gnat. "I was about ready to leave for the day."

"That's okay," Molly said quickly. "If you'll just tell me when you open in the morning, I'll come back then."

Mr. Bradbury said, "Ha," but he didn't sound amused. "I'm afraid the museum doesn't keep regular hours yet. Since I don't have an assistant, it's taking me forever to get things organized. I'm a teacher, and I only work here when I can. If the Lynnton Corporation paid me more than a pittance, this museum might have a chance of opening in the not-too-distant future."

"Oh. Well . . ." Molly tried to think of something to convince him to stay for a little. He was a grouch, but he was her only hope at the moment. "It's too bad about the pay," she said. "But you love this work, don't you? The woman at the Department of Records said you're a history buff."

"True." He peered at her again. "And are you one, too?"

"Not until I came here," Molly said. "I'm interested in the house we're staying in. It's the Caleb house."

"Andrew Caleb?" He suddenly looked interested. "That house?"

Molly nodded eagerly. "I really want to find out

66

all about it. When it was built and the people who lived there, from the very beginning. Do you think you might have some stuff on it?"

"Stuff!" Mr. Bradbury looked insulted as he gestured at the boxes in the hall. "This may look like 'stuff' to you, Miss . . ."

"Bishop," she said. "Molly Bishop. And I didn't mean it that way, like it was garbage. I'm really interested, Mr. Bradbury. Do you think you could help me?"

"My, you're persistent, aren't you?" Mr. Bradbury checked his watch. "I *do* have to go now. But I'll be here tomorrow, at about two o'clock. Come back then and I'll see if I can find the time. *If* you're still interested."

At exactly two the next afternoon, Molly went back to the museum.

"Amazing," Mr. Bradbury said when he saw her. "Someone under thirty who appreciates the past."

He sounded sarcastic, and Molly decided the best way to get his help was to be very serious about the whole thing. She was, anyway, so it wasn't hard to do.

Mr. Bradbury led her up the bare, squeaky stairs to a small, stuffy room with a tiny electric fan that didn't do much good. The room had more boxes, and file cabinets, and one lumpy easy chair.

"What you see here," he said, waving his hand

at the boxes and cabinets, "is the history of Lynnton. A year ago, the Lynnton Corporation asked me to organize the journals and letters that had been saved over the years. Not to mention the wooden dishes and old tools and furniture that you saw downstairs. But as I said, they pay me almost nothing. Most of their money went into the village. So it's an agonizingly slow process."

Molly looked around at the boxes and cabinets. Where would she even start?

But Mr. Bradbury seemed to know exactly where to start. He pulled open a file drawer and took out some plastic-covered papers. "The Caleb house goes back to at least the late 1600s, I think."

"Mr. Caleb thought it was built in the 1700s."

He made a sour face. "Mr. Caleb is wrong. I happen to be somewhat interested in that house myself. I simply haven't had the time to research it."

He looked at her sharply. "You never did tell me why you're so interested in it."

"I, ah . . ." Molly wasn't about to tell him about the girl. ". . . it's a history project," she said. "Sort of."

"Hmm. Well, I *do* know that Lynnton was founded in 1686. And Calebs helped found it." He tapped the papers. "So if you want to go back to the beginning, you start here."

"What are they, old newspapers?"

"Newspapers didn't get going in this country until 1705," he told her. He sounded like a teacher, and Molly remembered that he was one. "People communicated by word-of-mouth or in letters. These are letters, journals, even a few sermons."

"The actual ones?"

"Yes, and I suggest you handle them with extreme care." He sighed and clutched them to his chest. "I shouldn't really let you handle them at all. It's against my better judgment."

"I promise I'll be careful," Molly said. "Some of us people under thirty aren't total klutzes."

He frowned at her, but didn't comment. "Just one thing. Whatever you find, I insist you tell me. There may be some . . . well, never mind. Make sure you tell me, and only me."

Molly wasn't sure why he was making such a big deal out of it, but she agreed. Anything to get her hands on those papers.

Mr. Bradbury clutched the papers for another moment. Then he handed them to Molly as if he were giving her some rare jewels.

In a way, he was. As Molly tried to read the thin, yellowed pages through the plastic, she felt like she was really stepping back into the past, even more than when she went into the village. The village had been restored, but this was the real thing.

It was hard going at first. She had to get used

69

to the s's that looked like f's, and the old-fashioned way of saying things. But she slowly got better at it, and soon she was caught up in the lives of people long dead.

The shoemaker arrived this day read part of a letter dated May, 1689. *All were glad of his coming, as the harsh winter ruined many of even the stoutest shoes.*

Part of another letter said, *The rain having not ceased for two days, it was incumbent upon us to postpone the raising of Mr. Goodale's barn.*

Slowly Molly made her way through the old papers. She had just read about how everybody in the town gave up a day's labor to help fix the gristmill, when she finally caught the name of Owen Caleb. She was trying to decipher what it said when Mr. Bradbury poked his head into the room.

"I found something," she said excitedly, "about a man named Owen Caleb. He was the magistrate. Is that sort of like the mayor?"

"Sort of," he agreed. He stepped into the room, his small dark eyes gleaming with interest. "What did he do?"

Molly looked back at the paper. "He called a meeting. I can't make out the rest of it, it's too faded. But maybe there's more in here about him and his family."

"I'm sure there is, if he was the magistrate."

Mr. Bradbury was staring at her, his eyes like slits. "I have to run an errand," he said. "Can I trust you to hold down the fort?"

Molly just nodded. She was so engrossed in what she was doing that she didn't even hear him go. Owen Caleb had to be some great, great, great relation of Andrew Caleb. If she was lucky, maybe she'd find something else.

None of the papers were in order. Some were letters and sermons, like Mr. Bradbury said. And none of them were complete. Finally Molly found something that seemed to be part of a diary, and she found Owen Caleb's name again.

He'd traveled to Salem, one entry read. Another one told of him calling a meeting. Another said he'd had dinner at the journal writer's house. At last, Molly came across something she was looking for.

It was a different diary, she could tell by the writing. The entry was dated October, 1692. It said, *All of Lynnton helped to improve the roof of Magistrate Caleb's new house. The Woolrich house, being in great disrepair when Magistrate Caleb took it over, needs much work. But the new roof will afford good protection in the coming months.*

The Woolrich house, Molly thought. If it was the same house, then it had belonged to somebody named Woolrich before the Calebs took it over.

Why was the girl haunting it? Did she think it still belonged to her family? And what happened to the Woolriches? They must have moved away or something.

Molly looked through the stack of pages Mr. Bradbury had given her, but none of them seemed to match this one. She got up and went to the file cabinet, hoping to find more.

The first drawer didn't have anything, so she went on to the second. She thought she found something there, but when she compared the two, they didn't match.

Still holding the two pages, she started back to the file cabinet and jumped when she heard the dim rumble of thunder. Glancing up, she saw rain splashing against the window. The sky outside had grown so dark it seemed almost like nighttime in the house. She got up, switched on the overhead light, and was just about to open a drawer when she heard footsteps downstairs.

"Mr. Bradbury?" she called. "I found something about the Caleb house. Come see!"

There was no answer, so she called again. Still no answer. Just another clap of thunder. Then more footsteps.

Molly walked out to the landing and yelled down, "Mr. Bradbury! Come see what I found!"

The footsteps stopped, and then there was silence.

"Mr. . . ." Molly suddenly shut her mouth. It wasn't Mr. Bradbury down there. He would have answered. She was still holding the plastic-covered pages and she could feel her hands getting sweaty. If it wasn't Mr. Bradbury, then who was it? And why didn't they answer?

Suddenly the silence was broken. Not by footsteps. This time it was a voice. A dry, raspy voice that didn't belong to anyone Molly knew. But it knew Molly, because it was calling her name.

"Molleee," it said. "Molleee."

Molly's scalp prickled the way it had when she'd first heard the girl's voice. Her hands tightened on the plastic, but that was the only movement she made.

"Molleee," the voice called again. And then a long, lean shadow fell across the downstairs hall.

At that moment, the light flickered, and then a loud thunderclap shook the house.

That's when Molly moved. Without thinking about it, she stepped soundlessly across the landing and into the room across from the one she'd been in. She slipped behind the door and waited.

Another burst of thunder rattled the house. The light across the hall dimmed, grew bright, then finally went out for good. Squeezed behind the door, Molly held her breath and listened.

What she heard was a creak, then silence, then another creak. She knew that sound. She'd made

73

it herself, earlier. It was the creak of the stairs. Whoever had called her name was coming up.

Molly's heart was thudding in her ears. She had no idea what she was going to do. Right behind her, against the wall, was another easy chair. Turning slightly she lifted the cushion and put the pages under it. Then she straightened up and listened again.

"Mollleee." The voice was closer now and Molly had to bite her lips to keep from yelling. She closed her eyes and waited, hearing the footsteps slowly mount the stairs.

Two more creaks, and then they were on the landing. A pause, and they moved again.

Molly heard them hit the bare wood floor of the room she'd been in only moments before. Her eyes flew open, and she sped out from behind the door, dashed out to the landing, and raced down the stairs.

She didn't stop running until she reached home.

9

There was no way out of it: Molly knew she had to go back. For one thing, she really wanted to find out more about the family named Woolrich. For another, if she didn't tell Mr. Bradbury where she'd put those pages, he'd probably put her in the stocks. So she had to go back, even though just thinking about it made her hands start to sweat again.

Sam wanted to go with her. "You're not letting me do anything," he complained the next morning. "You told me about the ghost, but — "

"Ssh!" Molly hissed. They were just leaving the house, and Katherine was across the road, painting. "Will you please just not mention that word unless we're alone?"

"Sorreee," Sam muttered.

Katherine glanced up from the easel. "Hi. Off to town again?"

"Yep." Sam walked around to look at her work. "Hey! It's starting to look like something."

"But what? That's the question." Katherine wiped her forehead with the back of her hand and pointed the brush at the canvas. "What do you think, Molly?"

Molly stepped around and looked. The painting really was taking shape. Done in soft reddish-browns and grays, the house seemed lived in, as if the front door might suddenly open or a face might appear at the window.

"I'm glad you left out the bug light," Molly said.

Katherine smiled. "Yes, well, it just didn't seem to belong."

"It's nice," Molly said. "You're better than you said you were."

"Thank you."

"Are you going to sell it?" Sam asked.

Katherine laughed and wiped her forehead again. "No. I doubt that anyone would buy it, Sam. I'm really not that good. Besides," she added, "I'm doing this for the family. You two will have to help me find the right place to hang it when we go home."

A picture of their house flashed into Molly's mind then, with its gravel driveway and tall oak trees that her mother had loved but hated to rake up after. She hadn't thought of Ellen at all yesterday, but now she saw her clearly, wearing big work gloves and pulling a rake through the brown leaves. The house was behind her, white with dark blue shutters. Was there room in that house for a painting by Katherine?

Molly blinked and the image faded. "Come on, Sam. Let's go."

On the way into Lynnton, Molly managed to talk Sam out of coming with her to the museum. It wasn't hard. All Sam had to hear was that it was full of books and papers, and he lost interest. It sounded too much like school.

"I'll hang out in the village for a while and then get a Coke," he said. "But if that ghost comes back, you'd better tell me."

Molly promised and left him heading off toward the stocks.

It couldn't have been a ghost yesterday, she thought as she walked along. Maybe it was a robber. She guessed a robber might be after some of those old tools and dishes. But how would a robber know she was there, and know her name?

But a *ghost*? Did ghosts have shadows and climb stairs? Stupid questions. She believed in the girl, didn't she? So why not the raspy-voiced person she'd heard yesterday?

"Well, well." Mr. Bradbury's voice interrupted Molly's thoughts. He was standing in front of the museum. "I was wondering if you'd return."

"Hi, Mr. Bradbury." He was his usual sarcastic self, but he wasn't acting mad, just kind of surprised to see her. Maybe he didn't know what she'd done with the papers, Molly thought. Had she gotten lucky?

She had. As Mr. Bradbury unlocked the front door, he told her about coming back to find the electricity still off. And after yelling to make sure she wasn't still upstairs, he'd simply locked up and gone home.

The lights were back on this morning. "Ah, good," he said. "We'll be able to see the mess in all its splendor."

But Molly wasn't listening. While he was still talking, she dashed up the stairs and retrieved the old papers. Thank goodness they were still there, under the chair cushion. Holding them carefully, she went back downstairs and told Mr. Bradbury about the "visitor" the day before.

"Interesting," he remarked. He was sitting at his desk, his big feet propped up on the wastebasket. He was watching her carefully, his eyes narrowed to slits again. "Are you sure it wasn't just the product of an overactive imagination?"

"Mine, you mean?"

He raised his eyebrows and almost smiled. "Of course, yours. Who else was here? A trick of the mind, I'm sure that's what it was."

Molly wondered why he wasn't more worried about somebody breaking into the place. Did he really think she'd imagined the whole thing, like a six-year-old?

"I can't help wondering why you came back," he said. "If it was as frightening as you say, I'd think you'd want to stay as far away as possible." He took his feet off the wastebasket and leaned over the desk. "Unless you found something that brought you back. Did you?"

Molly remembered her promise — that she'd tell him first about anything she found. She still thought it was strange, but if she proved to him she was making progress, maybe he'd let her keep looking.

"Yes, I did find something," she said. She held out the page and showed him the passage about the Woolrich house. "Now I want to find out about the Woolrich family, because they lived there first. I couldn't find any more of this diary. But you've got lots of other papers. Could you let me look through them?"

Mr. Bradbury rubbed his long nose and looked at her. "I really don't think you'll find anything," he said.

"But I might," Molly said. What was his problem, anyway? Did he want her to stop? She thought he was interested in this, too. "I promise I'll be careful."

"Very well," he said finally. "I'll bring you some more, and I'll look in some other cabinets. It's a long shot, but maybe I'll find something."

In a few minutes he brought down some more

plastic sheets. Molly settled herself at Mr. Bradbury's desk and started in on them. None of them matched that first journal, but she couldn't just ignore them. They might have something important anyway.

Half an hour went by and she didn't find anything more about the people named Woolrich. She kept going back and forth, rereading passages, but she kept coming up with the same thing: nothing.

Suddenly Mr. Bradbury let out a shout. Then she heard him clumping quickly down the stairs.

"Woolrich, you said?" he asked, ducking his head as he came through the door.

"Right!" Molly jumped up. "Did you find something?"

For an answer, he held up a page and started to read. Molly could tell by the writing that it was from the same journal.

"On this fifteenth day of September, 1691, Master John Woolrich was buried. His wife, Sarah, and daughter, Rebecca, were much grieved. Indeed, all of Lynnton was."

Rebecca. Molly silently mouthed the name. Rebecca Woolrich. Was she the girl who cried so sorrowfully for her mother?

"It's like solving a puzzle, isn't it?" Mr. Bradbury asked. He looked excited by his discovery. Molly noticed he wasn't treating her like a six-year-old anymore. She couldn't figure him out at all. "The question is," he went on, "can we find all the pieces?"

"This is great," Molly told him. "Mr. Woolrich died in September, 1691, and the page I found yesterday says it was October of the next year when Owen Caleb moved into that house. I wonder what happened in between?"

"The missing pieces," Mr. Bradbury remarked. "Well, there are more papers upstairs. Of course, they're not in any sort of order."

"I don't mind," Molly said. "I have plenty of time to look."

"Unfortunately, I don't," he said. "I have to attend a teacher's conference. Come back tomorrow and we'll see what we can find."

Molly hated to stop now. But Mr. Bradbury wasn't coming back today, and she wasn't sure she wanted to stay there alone again anyway. As she stepped outside, she saw Sam trudging down the sidewalk, dragging a grimy piece of rope behind him.

"I'm starved," he announced. "Let's go home and have hot dogs."

They decided to take the path behind the village, and as they walked, Molly told him what she'd learned so far. "I don't know for sure that Rebecca's the girl," she said. "But I have this funny feeling she is."

81

"I have a funny feeling, too," Sam said. "This funny feeling that somebody's following us."

In spite of herself, Molly glanced back. All she saw was the tree-shaded path. "Come on, Sam, don't be dumb."

"I'm not!" Sam insisted. "There's somebody back there. I bet it's the other ghost — the one that scared you yesterday."

Molly sighed and shook her head. Maybe she shouldn't have told Sam anything at all. He just kept turning it into a game.

"You don't believe me," Sam accused her. "You think I'm just making — "

"Why don't you just be quiet, so I can listen?" Molly said. "If somebody's following us I'd never know, you're making so much noise."

Sam clamped his lips shut and they walked on silently.

That's when Molly heard it. A swishing, rustling sound, as if someone or something were moving through the high, thick bushes that lined the path.

"See?" Sam whispered. "There's someone back there." He shoved his glasses up and grinned. "The ghost!"

"Shut up!" Molly gave him a little push and they kept walking. She heard the rustle again and stopped. So did the sound.

Suddenly Sam shouted, "Yaahh!" and whacked

the piece of rope in the dust like a whip. "That'll get 'em!" Then he raced ahead.

Molly ran after him. She heard the pounding of her sneakers and the thump of her heart. But she heard something else, too: the swish-swish of the bushes as someone ran through them.

Sam stopped so quickly that Molly bumped into him. He went sprawling in the dirt, his glasses flying off his nose. "See what you did?" he yelled.

The glasses had fallen behind them, and as Molly went to pick them up, she saw it: a figure darting into the bushes back where the path curved. It was gone so fast, she only caught a glimpse of someone tall and thin, wearing dark clothes.

It might have been a trick of the light and shadow on the path, she thought. Except for one thing: Right after the figure moved, she heard the bushes rustling.

Sam was right. Someone had been following them.

10

I told you!" Sam said. "I told you there was someone back there!"

"All right, all right, you told me." Molly grabbed his arm and pulled him up. "Come on, put on your glasses and let's go." There weren't any storm clouds darkening the sky, there was no thunder or lightning to make her jump, but Molly was just as scared as she had been the day before. "Come on!" she said again.

"This is an evil ghost, I bet," Sam gasped out as they ran down the path. "It doesn't like what you're doing, so it's trying to stop you."

Molly didn't answer. She just concentrated on running.

Finally they reached the end of the path and came out on the road a few yards from their house. Panting, they stopped and turned around.

What they could see of the path was sun-dappled and empty. There was no wind, and not even the leaves were moving. Everything was quiet.

"I guess it dematerialized," Sam said.

He looked excited, and Molly could tell he still thought it was a game. A little scary maybe, but a game. She wasn't sure what to think, but she did know one thing: Ghost or not, it *wasn't* playing a game.

At dinner that night, Molly's father announced that he had to fly home for a couple of days to go over some things with his company. "Katherine'll take me to the airport day after tomorrow," he said, dishing out ice cream for everybody. "And when I get back, I think I'll finally have some time to enjoy Lynnton."

"Can I come to the airport with you?" Sam asked. "I need a break from this place."

Mr. Bishop laughed. "You want to see something modern? Sure, you can come. Maybe you should, too, Molly."

"I'd rather stay," Molly said. "I'll be okay by myself for a few hours."

"Not if you use the path," Sam said. Then he gave his best witch cackle.

Molly kicked him under the table.

"Why not?" Katherine asked. And Mr. Bishop said, "What path?"

"It's just a path that goes behind the town," Molly said. "It's . . ."

". . . full of poison ivy," Sam finished. He grinned at Molly. "It is, I saw it.'"

"Then stay away from it, please!" Mr. Bishop said. "Unless you want to spend the rest of the vacation covered in calamine lotion."

Molly agreed not to use the path. It was the last place she wanted to see for a while, anyway.

After dinner, Katherine and Sam went out into the yard to watch for lightning bugs while Molly and her father cleaned up.

"So," he said, "what do you think of Katherine's painting?"

"It's nice." Molly handed him the stack of ice cream dishes. "I told her that."

"You did?"

"Come on, Dad." She ran water into the sink and squirted in some soap. "I know she tells you everything I say. Or do."

"You know that, do you?" Mr. Bishop slid the dishes into the soapy water. "For your information, Katherine doesn't give me a daily report on your behavior. She *did* say, though, that you two seemed to have reached a truce. And she only told me that because I asked."

"Okay, I'm sorry," Molly said. Why did the grown-ups in a family always take each other's side? Even when her mother was alive, they used to do that.

"Well?" her father asked. "Is there a truce?"

"I guess so." Molly found a dish towel and started drying. "Anyway, we're real polite to each other."

"Well, a truce is better than a battle, I suppose," Mr. Bishop said. "But it sure does make for a weird family."

Funny, Molly thought. That's exactly what Sam had said.

Her father let the dishwater out and dried his hands. Then he put his hands on her shoulders and gave her a serious look. "I don't need to ask you to keep the truce while I'm away, do I?"

"Dad!" Molly squirmed away. "What do you think I'll do, throw a tantrum or call her nasty names or something? You asked me to be nice and I'm being nice."

"No, I asked you to try to treat her like part of the family," he said. "But being nice is a start, you're right." He tilted his head toward the living room. "Want to go out and help them look for lightning bugs?"

"Not now. I'm tired." Molly pushed her hair behind her ears and smiled. "I'm not trying to get out of it, Dad. I really am tired."

"Sure." He kissed her on the forehead. "See you in the morning."

By the time Molly took a shower and dried her hair, it had gotten dark outside. She put on a stretched-out tank top that was more comfortable than her pajamas, punched up the pillow on the bed, and tried to write another letter to Chris.

It was impossible. The only thing she wanted to write about was what had been going on. And what could she say about that? *Dear Chris, This sure is an exciting place. There's a ghost in my room and another one chased me home today.* Chris wouldn't believe it. She'd just think Molly was joking and Molly couldn't really blame her. This was the kind of thing you had to experience yourself.

"Hey, Mol!" She heard Sam's sneakers thumping up the stairs, and he burst into her room. The rope he'd found earlier was hanging from the back pocket of his shorts, and he was carrying a jar with holes poked in the lid. Three or four black bugs were crawling around inside.

"Look," he said. "Fireflies. I'm gonna keep them in my room tonight and watch 'em light up. It'll be neat."

"Mmm."

Sam tripped over the rope on his way to the bed and it fell onto the floor. "Hey. Are you mad at me?"

"Oh, no," Molly said. "You just practically told everybody about what happened today, that's all. After I asked you not to say anything."

"Sorry."

He did look sorry and Molly couldn't stay mad at him. After all, he hadn't heard the girl's voice, or seen her. How could he take it as seriously as she did?

"Never mind," she told him. "At least you remembered the poison ivy. I never even noticed it. I hope I don't get it."

"Yeah." He tossed the jar up, caught it, and headed for the door. "Maybe the evil ghost'll get it," he said as he left.

Molly tossed her notepad on the floor, flipped the pillow over, and leaned back, her arms behind her head. Was there really an evil ghost?

Except for that very first time, she'd never been frightened of the girl. Well, she *was* scared, a little. That was just because it was so strange, not because she had felt she was in danger. She had today, though. And yesterday, at the museum. But the spirit of Rebecca Woolrich had never made her feel like running.

Molly sat up straighter, remembering something Sam had said when they were running home earlier. "The evil ghost doesn't like what you're doing, so it's trying to stop you."

But all she was doing was trying to find out about Rebecca Woolrich and her mother. Why would anyone want to stop her from doing that? Who knew about it, anyway? Just Sam. And Mr.

Bradbury and Mr. Caleb. But Mr. Caleb seemed to have forgotten about it. And Mr. Bradbury was trying to help her. Or was he?

Molly remembered that figure on the path. Tall, wearing dark clothes. Like Mr. Bradbury. And when she'd told him about the shadow at the museum, he didn't seem to care. Was it him? Did he want to scare her? Did he not want her to find what she was looking for? Was he just pretending to go along with her?

It didn't make sense. If that was the way he felt, wouldn't he just tell her to get lost?

Unless, Molly thought, he wasn't sure what she'd find. So he was letting her look. But at the same time, he was scaring her, so she'd finally stop and then he could take over.

That made a little sense. He probably thought she'd give up once she got scared enough.

Molly shifted around some more and then tossed her pillow onto the floor. The sheet underneath was cool and she put her cheek on it, staring across the room at the side window. A moth flew up against the screen, attracted to the light from the landing. Molly closed her eyes and listened to it flutter. Her last thought before she fell asleep was that maybe she should just forget the whole thing.

When Molly got up in the morning, she decided not to go to Mr. Bradbury's. She still wasn't sure whether to give up trying to find out about Sarah and Rebecca Woolrich, or not, but it wouldn't hurt to stop for a while. It had been her idea to do the research in the first place; nobody had made her. She could stop whenever she wanted to. And she wanted to, at least for now. A crying girl-ghost was one thing. Being chased and scared out of her mind was completely different.

Katherine had other plans for the day, too. "The painting's almost finished," she said. "I *think*. What I need to do is stay away from it for a day or so and then go back to it with fresh eyes."

She was standing at the kitchen counter, blow-drying her dark, shoulder-length hair. "Your father discovered that Lynnton — the new part — has a municipal swimming pool," she went on, talking loudly over the whine of the dryer. "It's another steamy day, and a pool sounds like the best place to be. What about it?"

"Great!" Sam started gobbling his cereal. "Hurry up and eat so we can go, Molly!"

Molly didn't need any pushing. She couldn't think of anything better than spending a few hours in a cool swimming pool, far away from old journals and ghosts and raspy-voiced shadows.

The pool was a half hour's walk from Lynnton, but it seemed like a world away. It was hard to believe that the old village was close by, with its stocks and ducking stool, its meeting house and other ancient buildings, its women in long dresses and men in knee-length pants.

"This is more like it," Sam remarked when they got there.

Molly agreed. A crowded, noisy pool with a concession stand smelling of hot dogs *was* more like it. It was normal.

They stayed for almost four hours, and spent most of the time in the water. Even Katherine did. Molly thought for sure she'd be the type to oil herself with lotion and lie in the sun, but Katherine loved to swim.

Of course, she spent so much time swimming that she ignored everything else — like the fact that Sam had stuffed himself with five hot dogs.

"Five!" Katherine said when she found out. "Why on earth did you eat five?"

Sam was groaning and threatening to throw up. "Because I was hungry," he said, clutching his stomach.

Katherine shook her head at him. "But your stomach must have started hurting after the third one. Why did you eat two more?"

"I don't know," Sam moaned. "They just tasted good."

Katherine shook her head at him again. "Well, it's almost three. I suppose we've been here long enough anyway." She squeezed the water out of her hair and stepped into her flip-flops.

"I don't see why we have to go," Molly said. "His stomach's going to hurt just as much at home as it does here."

"I think the walk back to the house will help work off the hot dogs," Katherine said, gathering up towels.

Molly could have stayed for another two hours, at least. She wasn't tired at all. If Katherine had paid attention to Sam like a real mother, she would have noticed he was eating too much.

Molly shook *her* head this time. Katherine noticed, Molly knew she did. But she didn't say anything. She just handed Molly a wet towel and a bottle of sunscreen. "Ready?" Katherine asked politely.

"Ready," Molly said. Just as politely. The truce was still on.

Twenty-five minutes later, the three of them were on the dusty main street of the village. Sam was lagging behind, still making a big, loud deal about his stomach, and Katherine was walking with him. So Molly was ahead of them, by herself, when she saw the girl.

Rebecca Woolrich was standing across the road from the meeting house, in a small grassy square with benches around it. The benches were for tourists, but they were empty at the moment. Rebecca was alone.

The girl's head was bowed, and her hands were

over her face. Molly knew she was sobbing, even though there was no sound at all. Slowly Rebecca raised her head. Her hands slid down, over her cheeks and to her neck. Her fingers tightened against her throat, and her mouth opened in a silent one-word scream.

The word was "Mother."

11

When she felt the hand on her shoulder, Molly gasped and whirled away from it. But it was only Katherine.

"Molly?" Behind her pink-tinted glasses, Katherine's eyes were curious. "What is it?"

Molly just shook her head. Her eyes burned, as if she'd been crying along with Rebecca.

Katherine looked worried now. "Are you all right?" She reached out and felt Molly's forehead.

It was exactly what Ellen used to do when she thought somebody was sick. Molly closed her eyes, and for a second, the cool hand on her forehead felt just like her mother's.

"I'm the one who's sick," Sam grumbled. "If we don't keep walking, I'm gonna puke."

Katherine took her hand away and Molly opened her eyes. The feeling of comfort was gone. She looked back at the grassy square and saw that the girl was gone, too.

Molly didn't know if the feeling would ever come

back. But she was almost sure Rebecca would. Molly might want to give up the whole thing, but it seemed like Rebecca wasn't going to let her.

Rebecca did reappear, that night. Molly had fallen asleep early, tired from all the sun and swimming. When she woke, it was to the sound of Rebecca's voice.

It wasn't really night, it was early morning, and the sky outside was just beginning to lighten. The birds were probably starting to sing, but Molly couldn't hear them. Rebecca's voice drowned out every sound.

Wide awake, Molly stared toward the end of the room, where the voice was coming from. The sound was different this time. It was still sad, but there was another feeling to it. Urgency, that's what it was.

"Mother? What shall I do? I must right this terrible wrong. But how? Help me. Help me!"

Suddenly the voice sounded closer. Molly felt a puff of air on her skin as if someone had passed by. Then, in the middle of the room, she saw something.

At first it was like a shadow. Then gradually it took on a shape, and color. In a moment, the spirit of Rebecca Woolrich was standing there in her faded blue dress and tangled hair. Her eyes were open, and the tears slid down her cheeks and dripped onto her white collar. This was the first time Rebecca had actually appeared in the room.

Molly couldn't move, she couldn't even think. She only stared, eyes wide, as the girl sank to her knees in front of the rope Sam had dropped there the night before. Molly had tripped over it going to bed, but she'd been too tired to pick it up and toss it into Sam's room, so she'd left it.

Rebecca seemed to know it was there. She seemed to be looking at it, and suddenly, her sobbing grew louder and louder until Molly felt surrounded by it. It almost hurt to hear it and she knew she had to do something or she'd scream. She shut her eyes and put her hands over her ears, shaking her head back and forth to the rhythm of the voice.

"I'm sorry," she whispered. "I don't know what to do. I don't know what you want. I don't know what you're trying to tell me."

The crying didn't stop. Molly pulled the pillow over her head, but she still couldn't shut it out. It seemed impossible that everybody in the house didn't hear it.

Just when Molly thought she couldn't stand it any longer, that she'd have to run from the room to escape it, the crying broke off. There was a second of silence, and then a short, high-pitched shriek that echoed off the walls and rang in Molly's ears. After that, there was nothing except the chirping of the birds outside.

Molly pushed the pillow off her head and took a deep breath. It was over, for now. But she knew Rebecca would be back. Something had happened a long time ago that wouldn't let her rest. Some "terrible wrong." Today, Molly would start again, and try to find out what it was.

It was too early to do anything now, though, so Molly closed her eyes and let herself doze. The next thing she heard was the sound of the bathroom pipes clanging and gurgling. Her father was leaving today, she remembered sleepily.

She started to doze again and then she heard her door squeak as it was pushed open wider. Someone tiptoed in, sounding like a small elephant, and she knew it was Sam. The quieter he tried to be, the noisier he was.

"What do you want?" she asked, still not moving.

"My rope," he whispered. "I think I left it in here."

"You did," Molly told him. "I tripped over it last night."

"Sorry." Sam stopped tiptoeing and his bare feet slapped across the floor. "Hey, neat," he said.

"What?"

"The rope. Did you do this?"

Molly turned over and propped herself up on her elbows. Sam was standing right where Rebecca had been, holding the rope out and grinning.

Before Rebecca came, the rope had been stretched out across the floor like an uncoiled snake. Now it was curved and twisted at the top.

Still grinning, Sam slipped it over his head and pretended to gag.

A noose, Molly thought with a shiver. Rebecca had turned it into a noose.

At ten-thirty, Molly was standing in front of the museum. The new part of Lynnton was just starting to get busy. She saw people opening their shops and others hurrying toward cars. Andrew Caleb's Mercedes drove by in a flash of silver. She bet he was going out to the house to talk to the surveyors. Where would Rebecca go when the house was torn down?

At last she saw the tall, lanky figure of Mr. Bradbury coming down the sidewalk.

"My, my," he remarked when he saw her. "Already waiting, I see."

Molly nodded. "You said I could look through all those old papers, remember?" He was taking forever to get out his keys, and she shifted around impatiently.

Naturally he noticed. "No time for small talk, I take it," he commented, finally sticking the key into the lock. "You must be hot on the trail of something big."

Molly could have kicked herself. She didn't want him to know anything. "Well, not really," she lied. "I just . . . don't have anything else to do today."

"So you thought you'd spend your time in a musty room looking through ancient papers?" He narrowed his eyes, and she knew he didn't believe her. "Well, be my guest," he said. "In fact, I'm so fascinated by this single-minded interest of yours, that I think I may join you."

Molly's shoulders sagged. She didn't trust him and she didn't want him around while she was looking. What would he do if she found something?

But he'd already shrugged off his jacket and draped it on the coat tree. There wasn't any way she could stop him.

Just then, the door opened, and an older woman came in. "Oh, good," she said to Mr. Bradbury. "I was hoping you'd be in. I wanted to talk to you about those old dishes and tools we discovered in our barn. Now, I really think you should come out and take a look at them, but I brought a list just so you'll know what we have." She fished in her purse and brought out a notebook.

Mr. Bradbury gave her a sour smile. "Actually, Mrs. Perkins, I was just . . ." He looked at Molly.

"Oh, don't worry about me," Molly told him.

"I'll be fine by myself." Then she took off up the stairs, hoping that Mrs. Perkins would stay for a long, long time.

Half an hour later, Molly could still hear their two voices drifting up the stairs. She'd pulled out every piece of plastic covered paper she could find, and now she sat in the middle of the room, surrounded by them.

She picked up a page and squinted at it. The date was blurred, so she put it in the pile to read. That morning, on the way to the museum, she'd come up with her system: She'd start with the year 1691, any time after November, when Mr. Woolrich had died. If she didn't find anything in that year, then she'd go to the next. And maybe the next. So far, she hadn't discovered anything, but if it was in here, she was going to find it.

The time went on and the room got hotter. Molly got up and turned on the fan, then settled down again. She had no idea how much time had passed when she finally found more of the journal that had mentioned the Woolrich family. She recognized the writing on one page, then another and another.

This is it, she thought excitedly. Whoever wrote this journal talked about shoemakers and barn-raisings and births and deaths. Everything that had gone on in Lynnton, practically. She crossed her fingers, and started reading.

She never would have guessed what she would finally discover.

. . . now that the trouble in Lynnton has passed, the journal read. *A trouble that we pray will not be visited on us again, but of which we must be mindful. Who can know but what it will happen amongst us again, and who can fail to be . . .*

The sentence broke off at the end of the page. Frustrated, Molly turned the plastic sheet over, but the other side wasn't the right one. It had to be folded or something, she thought.

She peeled open the plastic and carefully eased the paper out of it. It *was* folded, and even more carefully, she spread it out and turned to find the rest of the story.

. . . and who can fail to be ever vigilant, it said. *'Twas the work of the devil, and we must pray that he has now been cast out from our midst, never to return.*

Every muscle tense, Molly kept reading.

All in Lynnton were gravely shocked. Mistress Woolrich, until these past months, gave every appearance of being a meek and virtuous woman. Yet behind this virtuous face, the very devil himself was working his will.

Many had heard of the troubles in Salem. Yet none believed it would be visited upon Lynnton.

102

Yet the trial of Mistress Woolrich proved it so.

Molly's heart was pounding. She was almost afraid of what was coming.

Indeed, the evidence was so strong, it was incumbent upon the elders and the magistrate to several times halt the proceedings until quiet was restored. And yet, who could blame the observers for their outcry? Three young girls, whilst under the tutelage of Mistress Woolrich, did fall to the floor in a most frightening swoon, and when they awakened, began to speak of choking, and of feeling chains upon their legs. The three accused Mistress Woolrich of being their tormentor. And even when taken from her presence, they continued to exhibit frightening symptoms, and cried that she was pinching and choking them. Days of fasting and of prayer by the village could not alter the facts. Who could doubt but that a diabolical hand was at work?

That hand, we must pray, has now been loosed. On this day, September 27, 1692, was Sarah Woolrich led to the gallows and hanged for a witch.

12

Molly's eyes filled, and she shivered in the small, hot room. There was more writing on the page, but she couldn't go on. She felt sick, and cold. A witch. They thought Sarah, Rebecca's mother, was a witch, and they hanged her.

She rubbed her hands up and down her bare arms, still shivering. She could hardly believe it. This morning, when she found the noose, had she known? In the back of her mind, had she suspected that Sarah had been hanged?

No wonder Rebecca cried. No wonder she couldn't rest, Molly thought. Her mother hadn't just died; she'd been murdered. The whole village thought she was a witch and they'd let her be hanged, so the "devil" would be cast out. But the only thing that had been cast out was an innocent life.

Molly was still sitting there, staring at nothing, when a shadow fell across the papers on the floor.

She jumped and looked around. Mr. Bradbury was standing in the doorway. She hadn't even heard him come up the creaky stairs.

"I came to see if you'd found anything," he said. "And I can tell by the look on your face that you have."

Molly knew there was no way to keep it from him. She was too upset to lie. Besides, he'd already moved into the room and was kneeling in front of the paper. She sat back on her heels and waited while he read.

After a few minutes, Mr. Bradbury sat back beside her. "Amazing," he said. "Absolutely amazing."

Molly rubbed her arms again and looked at him. "I think it's awful," she said. "I think it's one of the most terrible things I've ever heard of."

"Well, of course, it's terrible," he agreed. "Obviously the poor woman wasn't a witch."

He bent down and peered at the paper again. " '. . . the three young girls, whilst under the tutelage of Mistress Woolrich . . .' hmm, hmm . . . 'choking . . . chains upon their legs . . . pinching and choking.' "

Mr. Bradbury stopped and raised his eyebrows at Molly. "It's very much like what happened in Salem," he said. "You must have heard of the Salem witch trials."

Molly nodded. "It always seemed . . . unreal. Like a bad fairy tale."

"Unfortunately it was no fairy tale," he said. "Our journalist mentions Salem. The girls were sure to have heard of it and they must have been frightened and influenced by it somehow. Maybe Sarah Woolrich told them about it. Maybe she was acting strangely anyway, after her husband died, and that set them off. It's impossible to know now."

"One of them was named Elizabeth Caleb," Molly said.

"Yes, probably the magistrate's daughter." Mr. Bradbury sat back and rubbed his nose. "And Owen Caleb testified against Sarah Woolrich. Being the magistrate, I imagine his word carried a lot of weight."

Molly bent over the paper. "It says that before the hanging, Mr. Caleb told Sarah he'd pray for her soul. And she told him she was innocent and he should pray for his own." She couldn't help smiling. "I like that."

"Yes, so do I," he said. "I doubt that Owen Caleb lost much sleep over it, though."

"And then he moved into her house," Molly said indignantly. "He just took it over even though it wasn't his."

"Well, yes, but the owners were dead," Mr. Bradbury reminded her.

"Their daughter wasn't."

"Ah, yes, the daughter. What was her name?"

"Rebecca. I wish I knew what happened to her," Molly said. "This doesn't say anything and I haven't found any more of it."

He stood up, both his knees cracking. "She was probably bound out."

"What's that mean?" Molly asked.

"Well, she was alone and probably poor," he said. "So some family must have taken her in as a servant. It was common then, and it was a legal matter. She had to work for a certain number of years to earn her freedom."

"You make it sound like slavery."

"It was close," Mr. Bradbury agreed. "Some of the indentured children were treated terribly, others fairly well. And they could work their way free, at least."

It sounded awful to Molly. "But who would have taken care of all that after Sarah was hanged?"

"Someone in the village. Most likely the magistrate."

Owen Caleb again? Molly thought. Could he have been behind the whole thing, having Sarah accused of being a witch? Probably not, she decided. But he sure did take advantage of it. The man had been dead for hundreds of years, but Molly couldn't help hating him.

"Well!" Mr. Bradbury rubbed his hands together. "Now comes the fun part!"

"What fun part?"

He looked at her like she was slightly dim. "Telling everyone, of course! Making it known! Miss . . ."

"Bishop," Molly said. "Molly Bishop."

"Yes, Miss Bishop," he said with a nod. "Well, this is *news*, don't you realize that? It's going to put Lynnton on the map."

"It's already on the map," she reminded him.

"But not like it will be!" He was so excited she thought he might break into song. "It's a major discovery, you see. In Lynnton. And Salem thought it had the witch story all to itself."

"I don't think it's anything to be proud of," Molly said. "I mean, hanging an innocent person."

"Of course it's not," he agreed. "It was a shameful period. But it happened. And when this comes out, it's going to bring even more visitors here. More visitors mean more money. Who knows? Maybe the Lynnton Corporation will find it in their hearts to pay me enough so I can get the work done."

Money again, Molly thought. Was that all anyone cared about? What about Sarah? What about Rebecca? She wanted to shout the questions at him, but all she said was, "What are you going to do now?"

"Now?" He was carefully folding up the paper.

"Now I'm going to pay a visit to the Lynnton Corporation and let them know what I've learned." He cocked an eyebrow at her. "I can trust you to keep quiet about it, I hope. Until I've made my announcement?"

"Yes." Molly stood up and moved toward the door. "Maybe I'll come back later, or tomorrow, and find out what they said."

Out on the sidewalk, Molly watched Mr. Bradbury stride away. He had the precious papers tucked under his arm and he was whistling loudly. She turned in the other direction and walked slowly into the village.

He was happy, she thought. He didn't care about anything but how important this discovery was, and how much money it might bring. Well, it was nice that the discovery was so important, but that's not why she'd started looking in the first place.

She'd wanted to find out what had happened to Rebecca's mother, and she had. But it didn't make *her* happy. She was glad she knew, she guessed. But it was so awful it made her want to cry. It was bad enough to have your mother die. But to have her hanged as a witch? Molly could hardly imagine it. She wanted to stop thinking about it, but she kept seeing the words *led to the gallows and hanged for a witch*. Then the words would disappear and she'd actually see a woman, wearing a long dress, being led to a scaffold where a noose was hanging, maybe twisting around in the breeze.

Walking along with her head down, Molly heard footsteps pounding along the dirt road. She looked up and saw Sam running toward her.

"Hey, Molly!" he shouted. "Dad says to come home! We're leaving for the airport in fifteen minutes and he wants to say good-bye!"

Molly hurried up to him, and the two of them ran quickly back to the house. Her father was outside, putting his suitcase into the car. Molly wanted to tell him about Sarah Woolrich; she didn't care what Mr. Bradbury had said. But her father had on his "in a hurry" look, so she decided to wait. It wasn't the kind of story you told in a rush.

"There you are," he said when Molly ran up. "Sure you won't change your mind and come along for the ride?"

Molly gave him a hug, but she shook her head. "I'd rather stay," she said. She'd been cooped up in a musty room for hours. The last thing she wanted was a long drive in the car. "I think I'll just walk around or read or something, okay?"

"Sure." Mr. Bishop gave her one of his serious smiles. "I'll only be gone for a couple of days, but remember to keep an eye on Sam."

"I will."

"And" — he lowered his voice as Katherine came out of the house — "keep the peace, okay?"

"Right, Dad."

For a few hours, Molly had completely forgotten about Katherine. It was too bad she couldn't spend every day searching through old letters and journals. Keeping the peace was easy when the two of them were apart.

Her father, Katherine, and Sam got into the car, and Molly waved them off. Then she went into the house looking for something to eat.

Somebody had made tuna salad. Katherine — it had pickles chopped up in it. Molly made a face at it and took out a piece of chicken at least four dinners old.

Gnawing on this, she found a magazine and went out into the side yard. But she couldn't focus on the magazine. Her mind was still filled with old letters and pages from journals. The magazine's glossy pictures and up-to-date articles seemed unreal. She glanced up and saw the surveyors out in the field. She knew they weren't looking at her, but it felt like they were.

Molly went back inside, tossed the chicken into the garbage and the magazine onto the table. The surveyors, she thought suddenly. And then she knew why Rebecca kept coming back. Her home had been stolen, really, by Owen Caleb. This wasn't the Caleb House, it was the Woolrich

House. Sarah wasn't a witch, and she and Rebecca should have lived here for as long as they wanted.

What would Mr. Caleb — Andrew Caleb — do when he found out?

Something else was bothering her, though, and Molly wasn't sure what. Maybe it was just that she'd been concentrating so hard on finding out about Rebecca's mother, and now that it was over, she didn't know what to do with herself.

It didn't *feel* over, though, that was the problem. She had the funny feeling she'd forgotten something.

Molly shook her head. Thinking this way was dumb. So was hanging around the house. She rinsed her hands, brushed her hair, and walked into town. Maybe if she just walked around all afternoon, the funny feeling would go away.

It was hot, as usual, and even after just a few minutes' walk, Molly was sweating. She went into the meeting house and sat on one of the hard benches, letting the cross-breeze cool her off. Looking toward the front of the room, she half-expected to see Rebecca there again. But all she saw were other tourists.

Rebecca had been there, though. It was the second time she'd seen her, and then she'd followed her outside. Maybe this was where they had Sarah's trial, or tribunal, or whatever they

112

called it. Rebecca must have been there then, too.

Slightly cooler, Molly got up and went back outside. The well was crowded and she lined up to get a drink. Then she walked across the road and over to the small grassy square where she'd seen Rebecca yesterday.

The girl had stood there with her hands at her throat, and Molly suddenly realized that this must be where Sarah was hanged. Had Rebecca seen that, too?

Molly tried to make the image go away, but she couldn't. The woman, walking toward the scaffold. She must have been terrified. And the girl, Rebecca, watching, and crying, and sobbing for her mother. While everybody else watched and waited for Sarah to be hanged. For the devil to be cast out.

Molly shivered again and felt sick. She closed her eyes and rubbed them hard, until she made the image fade. When she opened her eyes, she saw that a group of tourists was sitting on the benches, drinking water and cider and trying to cool off. One of them, a woman, was looking at her curiously.

"Are you all right, honey? You look kind of woozy."

Molly shook her head. "I'm okay," she said. "I'm just hot." She turned and walked away, wondering what the woman would think if she told her what had happened on that spot so long ago.

Well, she'd know pretty soon, Molly thought. Mr. Bradbury was probably telling the story right now. Or maybe he was already finished and was calling all the newspapers about it. She asked someone for the time and found out it was almost three o'clock. He had to be done by now.

Curious about the Lynnton Corporation's reaction, Molly headed for the museum. Just before she reached it, she saw a man come out and walk away. Good. Mr. Bradbury had to be back.

She found him in his little office, sitting at the messy desk and staring at the ceiling.

"Hi," she said, stepping into the room.

Mr. Bradbury slowly lowered his head and looked at her.

"I came to find out what happened," Molly told him. "Were they excited? I bet they couldn't believe it at first. What did they say when you showed them the journal?"

He held up his hand. Then he cleared his throat. "Have you told anyone about it?" he asked.

"No, I said I wouldn't," Molly reminded him. "It's funny, isn't it, knowing something nobody else does? While I was walking in the village just now, I kept wondering what people would think if I told them." She moved a stack of magazines from a tall wooden stool and hitched herself up on it. "Anyway, what did they say?"

Mr. Bradbury cleared his throat again. "Nothing."

"You're kidding," Molly laughed. "You mean they were so surprised they couldn't say a word?"

He sighed and shook his head. "I mean, they said nothing. Because I told them nothing."

"You're kidding," she said again. Then she looked at him. "You're *not* kidding."

"No, Miss Bishop, I am not 'kidding' as you say."

"Well, why not? I mean, weren't they there or something?" But Molly could tell that wasn't what he meant. "Why not?" she repeated.

"I did some thinking on the way there," he said. Molly waited.

"A witch hanging." Mr. Bradbury cracked his knuckles. "It's such an unsavory subject."

"So?" Molly was getting impatient.

He frowned at her from under his dark eyebrows. "Please, don't use that tone of voice with me."

Holy cow! This morning he'd been acting so happy, whistling and everything. Now he sounded like an angry parent.

"I'm sorry," Molly said. "I just don't get it."

"There's nothing to 'get,' Miss Bishop," he said.

"I simply decided that a story so distasteful will put Lynnton in a bad light. We're a new tourist attraction and we don't need that kind of publicity."

Mr. Bradbury pushed back his chair and stood up. "Now, if you'll excuse me, I have to be going."

13

"Wait a minute, please!" Molly jumped off the stool and went over to the desk. "What you said — it doesn't make sense!"

"It makes perfect sense to me."

"But it can't! I mean, just this morning you said the story was going to put Lynnton on the map and everything," Molly argued. "You were talking about how more people would come here and there'd be lots more money for your museum. Don't you remember?"

"That was just the excitement of discovery talking," Mr. Bradbury said. "As I told you, I had second — and wiser — thoughts."

"I don't think they're wise." Molly put her hands on her hips and shook her hair out of her eyes. "I think they're dumb."

She knew she was being rude, and she thought for sure Mr. Bradbury would tell her not to use that tone of voice again. Instead, he shoved his hands in his pockets and turned to face the window, his back to her.

"I think you'd better go now, Miss Bishop," he said.

Molly let out a long, frustrated breath and headed for the door. Then she stopped and turned around.

"If you won't tell, I will," she said. "I was the one who found out about it. I was the one who wanted to look for it. I can tell about it if I want to."

"Certainly," he agreed. "Just remember one thing."

"What?"

"I have the documents," he said, still not turning around. "Without them, I'm afraid no one will believe a word you say."

Furious and frustrated, Molly left the museum and practically stomped back into the village. All that work, all that time looking through ancient pieces of paper! And *he* all of a sudden decides not to say anything about it! Just like that!

The worst thing about it was that he was right. Molly could tell every tourist in sight about Sarah Woolrich and it wouldn't make any difference. *He* had the stupid documents!

No, the worst part about it was what she'd said before: It didn't make any sense. Nobody just changed their mind like that, not without a good reason. And Mr. Bradbury's reason was lousy.

"Distasteful story." Ha! People *loved* stuff like that. Look at the way they slowed down for car accidents and read gossip magazines. Look how they took pictures of themselves in the stocks and laughed at the ducking stool.

Mr. Bradbury was lying; Molly knew it.

When she got to the grassy square, Molly stopped and slumped down on one of the benches, trying to think of what to do. When her father came back, she'd tell him what she'd discovered. He knew the people at the Lynnton Corporation. He could convince them she wasn't making the whole thing up. She wished she'd told him earlier; now she'd have to wait.

Molly leaned her head back and stared at the puffy white clouds. The most important thing was telling Mr. Caleb. If he knew it wasn't really his house, maybe he would give it to the village. It wasn't *his* fault, of course, but his ancestors had practically stolen the house. He'd understand, wouldn't he? Or would he say it was such a long time ago, it didn't matter? Molly hoped not. Because how could she tell him about Rebecca? How could she make him believe in a ghost?

Molly knew she couldn't. All she knew was the house belonged to Rebecca. They'd killed her mother and taken her home, and Rebecca couldn't rest until things were put right.

When Dad comes back, Molly thought, I'll tell

him everything. And together we'll tell Mr. Caleb.

She got up and walked on, out of the village and onto the road toward her house. She was hot and itchy and decided to take a shower when she got back. Maybe it would cool off her temper, too.

Several yards away from the house, Molly came to the place where the path veered off from the road, the path she and Sam used to take. She stopped and looked at it.

That was it. That's what had been bothering her all day, at least before Mr. Bradbury did his big switch. Sam's evil ghost.

Was it Mr. Bradbury? It seemed awfully crazy for him to pretend to go along with her and try to scare her off at the same time. But everything that was going on seemed crazy.

Why didn't he want anyone to know about Sarah Woolrich? Was it money? Maybe he wanted to sell the story or something, and get famous and rich. Maybe he thought the Lynnton Corporation would take over, and he wouldn't make a penny out of it.

Molly didn't know. But she was going to find out, just as soon as her father got back. Puffing out a breath of air, she walked on to the house.

Letting herself inside, she headed straight for the bathroom and stayed in the shower long after the hot water ran out. Then she wrapped one towel around herself and another around her hair and padded barefoot out to the kitchen.

The contents of the refrigerator hadn't changed. The only thing to eat was tuna salad, ruined by pickles. Molly settled for a box of crackers and the last Coke and went upstairs.

The rope was still twisted into a noose, and it was still lying in the middle of the floor where Sam had dropped it after he had pretended to hang himself. The sight of it made her sick.

Molly grabbed it up, untied it, and threw it across the hall into Sam's room. Mr. Bradbury was right about one thing: It was an unsavory business. She didn't want to think about it anymore.

She put on a clean pair of shorts and a loose, mint-green T-shirt. Then she aimed the fan at the bed and settled down with the crackers and Coke.

Molly tried to think of other things. She tried to imagine what Chris was doing back home, and what seventh grade would be like. She looked at the picture of her mother and tried to remember things they'd done together.

Nothing worked. Her mind kept going back to Rebecca and Sarah and Mr. Bradbury. And why, why, why?

Maybe the radio would help. She reached down to where she kept it, on the floor by the bed, and . . . her fingers froze on the switch. What was that?

A sound, like someone stepping on a creaky floorboard.

Molly shook her head. There was nothing strange about creaky noises in this house. It moaned and groaned and squeaked all the time, all by itself.

She lifted the radio up onto the bed and started to turn it on again. And stopped again.

Another creak. Just the old house, Molly thought. But she didn't turn the radio on.

Instead, she got her pad and a pen and decided to write a letter to Chris. She needed to tell somebody about all this. She should have done it before. Chris was her best friend; she wouldn't think Molly was crazy. Maybe she'd even have some ideas about what to do.

Dear Chris, she wrote, *The weirdest thing happened today. Actually, it didn't start today. It started a couple of days after we got here.*

Did I tell you about this house we're staying in? It's really old. I mean really old. And — don't laugh — it's haunted!

You know what it's like when you're alone in the house, and you get the strange feeling that you're not alone? Well, in this house . . ."

Molly stopped, the pen poised above the pad.

She hadn't heard anything this time. But the feeling she'd been writing about — the feeling that she wasn't alone — was suddenly true.

Was it Rebecca? Molly waited, listening for the girl's voice. But nothing came. She looked toward the end of the room, but all she saw were some very real dust balls.

Except for the soft hum of the fan, there was no other sound in the house. But the feeling of not being alone was so strong she couldn't shake it.

Carefully she eased herself off the bed and stood, listening. Then she moved slowly across the room and shut the fan off. As it spun to a stop, she thought she heard something else. A soft, shuffly sound, like a curtain blowing in the wind. Or someone walking quickly and quietly in stocking feet.

Molly's mouth went dry and her heart speeded up. Had she locked the front door? She couldn't remember, but her family almost always left it unlocked except at night. So she probably hadn't. It wouldn't matter anyway. If someone wanted to get in, there were always the windows. Low ones. And the side door in the living room.

Molly could feel little drops of sweat on her forehead. She was scared. She was so scared. She'd never felt like this with Rebecca. The only other time she'd been this scared was at the museum, when she saw the shadow and heard the voice calling her name.

But nobody could be trying to scare her now. There wasn't any reason. If it had been Mr. Bradbury that day at the museum and on the path, it couldn't be him now, could it? He had what he wanted.

For a few long moments, Molly stood by the fan and listened to her heart thud. But that was all she heard. She'd been holding her breath, and now she let it out, slowly. Her leg itched; she had to scratch it. She had to move, even if it was just to the bed. Or *under* the bed.

She'd taken two steps when she heard it.

"Mollleee."

The same voice, dry and raspy, like somebody with a bad sore throat. The same voice, calling her name.

"Mollleee."

Sam's evil ghost. She hadn't believed in it. But somebody was in the house. Somebody who knew her name.

Molly was so scared she wanted to cry. If she heard that voice one more time, she knew she'd scream.

"Mollleee."

Before she screamed, Molly raised her foot and stomped down on the floor as hard as she could.

And she didn't really scream, she shouted.

"Stop it! Go away! Leave me alone!"

Now she *was* crying. She looked around and saw the tall, old-fashioned wardrobe that she used for a closet. She was almost to it when she heard a door bang open downstairs.

Then she did scream.

14

Molly was scrambling into the wardrobe, pushing aside clothes and hangers, when she heard footsteps pounding up the stairs. Then she heard *other* voices calling.

"Molly? Molly!"

"Hey, Mol!"

Katherine's voice. And Sam's.

She squirmed back out and pushed her yellow windbreaker off her head just as the two of them burst into her room. She thought she'd never be glad to see Katherine, but at that moment, she almost felt like hugging her.

"Mol, we heard you yelling!" Sam said excitedly. "What is it, a rat or something?"

"It was . . ." Molly gulped back some tears and wiped her cheeks. She was so shaky with relief, she couldn't seem to get back on her feet. "I heard . . ."

Katherine came quickly across the room and helped her up. Her dark eyes were wide and worried. "What, Molly?"

Molly took a few deep breaths. "I thought . . . I mean, there was somebody in the house," she said. "I was up here and I heard these noises downstairs. First I didn't think it was anything, but then it started — "

"I'm gonna go see!" Sam said, heading for the door.

"Sam!" Katherine let go of Molly's arm and reached for him.

"I just wanna — "

"Sam!" Molly yelled.

And then they all jumped. Downstairs, a door had screeched open and banged against a wall.

"That was the side door," Katherine said. She looked scared, but she looked mad, too, and she went out to the landing. "You two stay here!" she called back over her shoulder.

They heard her trot lightly down the stairs, slowing down a little when she reached the bottom. Sam raced across the landing to his room and was back in a couple of minutes.

"I can see the yard from my window and it's empty," he reported. "Except for Katherine. She's walking around with my baseball bat."

Molly wasn't sure a bat would do any good.

Sam spotted the Coke and took a sip. "Who was it, Mol?"

"How should I know?" she asked. "I was up

here the whole time. I didn't see him, I just heard him. Or her."

"Or IT!" Sam's eyes widened. "Oh, wow, I bet *that's* what it was!"

Before Molly could answer, Katherine's voice was calling. "It's okay to come down now. Whoever it was is long gone."

Sam rushed out of the room and Molly went after him. In the kitchen, Katherine had just put the bat down and was going for the telephone. "I don't think the police will find anyone," she said, "but I'm going to report this anyway."

"It won't do any good!" Sam was almost jumping up and down. "The police can't do anything about a ghost!"

Katherine stopped punching the numbers and looked at him. "Sam, it wasn't a ghost."

"Yes, it was!"

"Sam," Molly said.

"It was, I know it was," he yelled. He looked scared and excited at the same time. "It was the same one that followed us on the path!" He was much too keyed up now to remember that what he was saying was supposed to be a secret, and he started blurting things out right and left. "See, this one, the one that was in the house and on the path? That's the bad one. But there's a good ghost, too. Molly saw it and it's a girl and she came to Molly's room and . . ."

This time, Molly shouted his name. But it was too late. Katherine hung up the phone and looked back and forth at the two of them.

The look on Katherine's face made Sam stop, finally. He scratched his head and shrugged his shoulders. "Well, it's true," he said more calmly. "Ask Molly."

Molly couldn't think of any way out of it. She swallowed and said, "Some weird things have been happening."

The first thing Katherine said was, "Let's sit down."

In silence, they pulled out chairs and sat at the sturdy wooden table. Molly fiddled with the pages of the magazine she'd left there earlier. She knew Katherine was waiting, but she didn't even know how to start.

As if she'd read Molly's mind, Katherine said, "Why don't you begin at the beginning?"

Molly took a deep breath. "It started with Rebecca," she said. "Rebecca Woolrich."

By the time Molly had finished talking, the light had changed. It still wouldn't be dark for a while, but the sun was on its way down. The kitchen was getting dim, but when she stopped, nobody got up to turn on a light.

In fact, nobody had moved much at all while she'd been talking. Even Sam hadn't fidgeted or wandered off to see what was on television. Which was really amazing. But then she remembered that he didn't know the whole story.

Molly put her chin in her hands and kept her eyes on the table. She was almost afraid to look at Katherine. It had been easy to tell how she'd tried to find out about the house, and about looking through all the old papers. But the part about Rebecca was hard. Telling Sam had been different — she knew he'd believe her. But Katherine? What was Katherine going to think?

If she laughs, Molly thought, or if she says I must have imagined the whole thing, I'll never speak to her again. Finally she raised her eyes and looked across the table.

"I know you don't believe me," she said.

Katherine took a big breath. "I'm not sure that matters." She bent forward, clasping her hands together on the table. "I can't pretend I understand, because I've never had an . . . experience like that. But I do believe you didn't dream it or make it up." Leaning back in the chair, she stretched her long legs out and tilted her head, smiling a little. "Okay?"

"Okay." Molly leaned back, too, feeling relieved. Katherine hadn't laughed or made her feel dumb. That was all she could ask for. And Katherine was acting pretty calm about it, too. Molly wasn't sure that her father would have had the same reaction, and she was actually glad he wasn't around at the moment.

No one said anything else for a minute, but the mood around the table seemed to change. It didn't feel like they'd been talking about ghosts and witch hangings and scary voices. It felt relaxed, like they'd been playing cards or just hanging out together.

Sam was the first one to break the silence. "I'm starved," he said. "What's for dinner?"

"The groceries!" Katherine scraped back her chair and stood up. "Sam, they're still in the car; we completely forgot about them. Come on, let's get them in and eat something."

While Sam and Molly lugged in the sacks of food, Katherine set the table with paper plates. It was still hot, too hot for cooking, so they ate the tuna salad, taco chips, and cheese and fruit. Molly was into her second helping of tuna salad before she realized it was the one with the pickles. She started to push it aside, then changed her mind. It wasn't *that* bad.

"This is like a picnic," Sam commented, pouring himself some more soda.

"It is," Katherine agreed. "Except instead of games afterward, we're going to have a strategy session."

"Huh?"

"We're going to plan what to do," she explained.

"About what?"

"About what's happened." Katherine started gathering up the paper plates and cups. "You didn't think we were just going to forget it, did you? Like Molly said, some weird things have been going on, and I think we should do something about it."

Molly had been putting the lids back on the salad containers. Now she stopped. "You really think there's something we can do?"

"Yeah," Sam said. "How can you fight a bunch of ghosts?"

"Sam." Katherine finished tying up a garbage bag and looked at him. "We're talking about two different things here. One is Molly's experience with Rebecca Woolrich. The other is what you call the 'evil ghost.'"

"Right."

"I think the two things are connected," she said. "But I don't for a minute believe there's an evil ghost."

"I don't, either," Molly said. "I almost did, especially today. But it's all wrong. Rebecca didn't scare me."

"Rebecca didn't slam doors and crush the grass with big feet, either," Katherine pointed out.

"You found footprints?" Sam asked.

"Out in the side yard," she told him. "I suppose someone else could have made them, but I doubt it. Anyway, whoever it was is very much alive."

Sam looked disappointed. "Okay, but if it wasn't an evil ghost, then who was it?"

"Mr. Bradbury?" Molly said to Katherine. "I told you how he acted. Do you think it's him?"

"I don't know," Katherine said thoughtfully. "If it is, then he belongs on the stage. Pretending to be so enthusiastic about your search, and secretly trying to stop you at the same time? It would take a really good actor to do that."

"That's what I thought," Molly said. "But he's the only one who knows everything that's been going on."

Katherine nodded. "He's got some questions to answer, that's certain."

"You're going to talk to him?"

"I sure am. Nobody's going to frighten my children and get away with it." Katherine crossed her arms and frowned. "I want to get to the bottom of this, and Mr. Bradbury's the best place to start. He may not be Sam's evil ghost, but he knows more than he's telling."

"Maybe he's scared to tell," Sam said. "I thought there was an evil ghost. Maybe he does, too."

"I don't — " Katherine broke off and looked at him. Then she smiled. "Well. You might be right, Sam. You just might be right."

* * *

Later, Molly lay in bed, thinking things over. Her father had called to tell them he'd had a safe trip, and Molly thought for sure Katherine would blab the whole story to him. But she hadn't. She even made Sam promise not to say anything before she gave him the phone.

It was almost like she understood that Molly wanted to be the one to tell him everything. When she was ready.

Molly wasn't sure when that would be. It had been hard enough telling Katherine. But Katherine had surprised her, she had to admit it. She didn't even mind when Katherine had called them *her* children. It sounded strange, but after what had happened earlier, it actually made her feel safe.

She turned over and looked at the picture of her mother. She wished Ellen were here, right now, so she could tell *her* everything. She wondered what she'd think about it.

But Molly was too tired to stay awake wondering for long. The day felt like it had gone on forever, and besides, there was tomorrow to think about. Tomorrow, Katherine said, they were going to start digging until they got to the bottom of it all.

Tomorrow was going to be a very interesting day.

15

When Molly came downstairs the next morning, Katherine was just finishing a telephone conversation. It sounded like business. She was dressed for business, too, in a light-brown suit and high heels.

"I'd like to get the information tonight," Katherine said. "But if you don't have time to get back to me, please call me tomorrow morning. What?" She laughed. "No, I'm not thinking of joining another firm. This is a private matter. But it's very important."

Katherine's hair was already dry, so Molly made some toast. It was impossible not to overhear, and she couldn't help worrying. Had Katherine already forgotten what they were going to do today?

In another minute, Katherine hung up and turned to Molly. "When do you think Mr. Bradbury will be there? I can't wait to get to the bottom of this."

Molly stopped worrying and bit into her toast. "I'm not sure," she said around a mouthful. "I don't think he has any regular times. I guess we could call."

Katherine thought about it and shook her head. "I'd rather just show up," she decided. "Take him by surprise. If he's not in when we get there, then we'll just camp on the doorstep."

"He'll be surprised to see *you*, that's for sure." Molly looked at Katherine again, then looked down at herself. Flowered shorts and an orange T-shirt. And flip-flops. "I think I'll change my clothes," she said. "Maybe he'll take me more seriously if I'm not wearing shorts."

"It's up to you," Katherine told her.

"But that's why you're dressed up, isn't it?"

Katherine nodded. "I'm not sure why I even brought this suit," she said. "I only use it for business."

"Well, this is business," Molly said, and went upstairs to change.

All she had were her denim skirt, a cotton blouse, and a pair of leather sandals. They weren't exactly businesslike, but she didn't feel so much like a little kid in them.

Sam was eating cereal when Molly got back downstairs. "I'll be ready in a minute," he said.

Molly's shoulders slumped. Sam couldn't come

with them. She knew he'd either get bored or else he'd start talking about ghosts again. It wasn't his fault; he was only eight. But Mr. Bradbury would never tell them anything if Sam was around.

"Um, Sam — "

"Sam," Katherine broke in. She'd just come out of the bedroom with a handful of envelopes. "I need your help. These letters are kind of important. Could you take them to the post office while Molly and I are with Mr. Bradbury?"

"I wanted to come, too," he said.

"I know, but listen." She plopped the envelopes down next to his bowl. "It isn't fair, but you just can't come. Molly and I wouldn't mind, but from what Molly said about him, I know Mr. Bradbury would."

Sam thought it over. "I guess you're right," he decided. "Molly said he's a real grump. He probably hates kids." He thought some more. "But what am I supposed to do? I don't want to stay here."

He didn't say "by myself," but Molly knew that's what he meant.

"No," Katherine agreed. "After the post office, just come to the museum and wait outside."

Sam looked at the envelopes. "Are these really important?" he asked suspiciously.

Katherine laughed. "Yes, they're really important. They're not a bribe to keep you out of the way." She picked up her purse and took out a couple of dollar bills. "After the post office, you can buy yourself an ice cream if you want. *That's* the bribe."

Out of the corner of her eye, Molly snuck a look at Katherine. When had she learned how to handle Sam?

"We're in luck," Katherine said when they reached the museum a little later. "It's open."

Now that they were there, Molly felt nervous, not lucky. What was Mr. Bradbury going to say when they came marching in? What would he do? For all she knew, he might call the police and have them thrown out.

"You don't mind if I do some of the talking, do you?" Katherine asked. "I thought about it a lot during the night, and I have a couple of things I'd like to say to him."

"Are you kidding?" Molly said. "You can do all the talking if you want. I said everything I could think of yesterday."

"Well, look, let's not go in expecting the worst," Katherine said. "Who knows? Maybe he got up on the right side of the bed this morning. Ready?"

"Ready."

Mr. Bradbury was in his office, and the minute

he saw them, Molly knew he'd gotten up on the wrong side.

"Miss Bishop."

"Mr. Bradbury." Molly tried a smile, but she didn't get one back. She gestured at Katherine. "This is . . ." Molly stopped. She couldn't call her mother. She'd always called her "my father's wife," but that sounded funny all of a sudden. Besides, both expressions made her feel so young, like she'd run home to mommy for help.

Katherine stepped forward and held out her hand. "Katherine Edelman, Mr. Bradbury. I'm a lawyer."

He raised his eyebrows and let go of her hand. "Miss Bishop's lawyer?"

"You could say that," Katherine told him. "I'd like to discuss something with you." She looked over her shoulder at the display room. Nobody was in it. "You can spare some time, can't you?"

"Some." He put his hands in his pockets and his elbows stuck out like a wire coat hanger. "I'd ask you to sit but I'm sure this won't take very long."

"I hope not." Katherine smiled. "I think you probably know why we're here."

"Yes, I imagine it has to do with what happened yesterday." He glanced at Molly. "Am I right, Miss Bishop?"

Molly nodded. "I told Ka . . . Ms. Edelman about it."

"I gathered that," he said. "What I don't understand is why."

"Because she was still confused about why you changed your mind," Katherine told him. "And so am I, frankly."

To Molly, Katherine sounded very friendly, like she was just trying to get things straight. Mr. Bradbury must have felt the same way because he took his hands out of his pockets and leaned back against the desk.

"You see," Katherine went on, "Molly told me how much you seem to love your work and how enthusiastic you were when she made her discovery."

"I was," he agreed. "I still am. But as I explained, it won't do Lynnton any good. People won't come to see a seventeenth-century village; they'll come to see where a supposed witch was hanged."

"As long as they come, does it matter why?" Katherine perched on the stool Molly had sat on yesterday. "Molly said one of the reasons you were so excited was because of the extra money more tourists would bring."

"I'm not in this cramped little museum for the money," he said. "I'm here because of my love of history."

"Exactly," Katherine said. "And Molly uncovered a piece of history that's been buried for hundreds of years. But you want to bury it again. That doesn't sound like a history lover to me."

Mr. Bradbury's long, horsey face flushed. He straightened up and said, "I really don't see the point to this, Ms. Edelman. I have my reasons for doing what I did. If you don't understand them, I'm sorry."

He walked around behind the desk and pulled out the chair. "If you'll excuse me, I have an enormous amount of work to do."

But Katherine wasn't finished. She stood up and walked over to the desk. Mr. Bradbury had started to sit, but he stopped.

"There's another reason why we're here," she told him. "Yesterday, in the late afternoon, someone broke into our house while Molly was there, alone. It wasn't your typical break-in, because whoever did it called Molly's name."

Katherine put her hands on the desk and leaned closer to him. "It happened just after she told you that she'd go to the Lynnton Corporation herself," she said. "It was done on purpose to frighten her. And it was an ugly, cowardly thing to do."

Molly couldn't see Katherine's face, but her voice was cold and hard. Katherine was furious.

Mr. Bradbury's jaw dropped and his face got red again. He swallowed hard and looked at Molly. He looked scared.

"I understand why you're angry," he said. He

had to clear his throat before he went on. "But I assure you — both of you — that I had nothing to do with that. I have faults, but threatening children isn't one of them."

Katherine stayed where she was for a minute, staring at him. Then she said softly, "I hope not, Mr. Bradbury."

Ten seconds later, Molly and Katherine were back outside. Sam wasn't there yet, so they had to wait.

"Well," Katherine sighed. "That didn't come out the way I hoped."

"Do you think he was the one?" Molly asked. "The one in the house?"

Katherine shook her head. "No. What about you?"

"I don't think so, either," Molly said. "When you told him about it, he looked totally surprised. I guess he could have been lying, but I believed him."

"So did I. He also looked scared, I thought."

"Me, too!" Molly agreed. "That was weird, wasn't it?"

"Mmm." Katherine stared down at the sidewalk, thinking for a minute. Then she gave herself a little shake. "Well, at least we can go back and get out of these clothes. Then we'll have to decide if there's anything else we can do."

She put her hand out and touched Molly's shoulder. "I'm sorry, Molly. I wanted to do better than that."

"It wasn't your fault," Molly told her. "I thought you did good. Really good."

Katherine smiled and took her hand away. "Thank you, Molly."

They saw Sam then, coming down the sidewalk with a double-dipper in his hand. He started running when he spotted them. "Hey!" he shouted. "What happened? Did he confess?!"

Molly and Katherine went to meet him halfway. "No confession, I'm afraid," Katherine said. "Let's go home and we'll give you all the details."

"Was he mean?" Sam asked. "And grumpy, like Molly said?"

"Not too grumpy." Katherine thought of something and laughed. "Molly, you told me a lot about Mr. Bradbury, but you didn't mention that he looks exactly like Ichabod Crane."

Molly laughed, too. "He does, I know. Especially when you told him what happened yesterday. He looked like the Headless Horseman was after him!"

"I knew it!" Sam said. "He's scared, isn't he?"

"I think he is," Katherine agreed. "I think he's very scared."

They were passing the museum again, and as they did, Molly glanced up at the window. The tall, lanky figure stepped back quickly, but not before she saw him. Mr. Bradbury had been watching them.

16

After they got home and changed clothes, Katherine made some cheese sandwiches and a big pitcher of iced tea. They took their lunch out to the yard, and Molly and Katherine told Sam what had happened with Mr. Bradbury.

"Why don't you do what you said you'd do?" he asked Molly. "Tell everybody about it anyway?"

"You could, you know," Katherine said. "I'd certainly stand up for you."

"Thanks," Molly said. "I already decided to tell Dad when he comes back. Maybe if all three of us go to the Lynnton Corporation, they'll listen."

"Yeah, then you'll be famous," Sam said.

Katherine smiled. "I don't think that's what Molly's interested in."

"Right, I'm not," Molly agreed. "I mean, it's kind of exciting, finding out something that nobody else knows. But if that's all it was, I wouldn't care about telling people." She stood up and walked around the overgrown yard. "It's Rebecca, see? She lost her mother. She needs to know her home isn't going to be lost, too."

Katherine started to stay something, but the phone rang and she went inside to answer it. When she came back out, she started to say something again. But then there was a knock at the front door and she went to get that.

When she came back out this time, she wasn't alone.

"Mr. Bradbury?"

"Miss Bishop."

Sam's mouth dropped open.

"I wonder," Mr. Bradbury said, "if I might have some of that tea. I think it might be easier to say what I have to say if my throat's not so dry."

"Of course." Katherine poured him a cup. "Why don't you sit down?" she said, waving at the fourth chair.

"Thank you. That might make it easier, too." He sat and drank the tea in one long swallow.

Sam watched him warily. To him, Mr. Bradbury was the bad guy.

"Now." Mr. Bradbury set the paper cup in the grass and looked at Molly. "Miss Bishop, I owe you an apology."

Molly had been standing, but now she sat down so hard the chair almost collapsed. Apologies from grown-ups were as rare as snow in July. One from Mr. Bradbury was like a blizzard.

"As you know," he went on, "after you discovered what happened to Sarah Woolrich, I went off to tell the Lynnton Corporation about it."

Molly nodded. "But you changed your mind."

"No. The truth is, I didn't change my mind."

"You mean you told them?"

"I told one of them," he said. "He was surprised, naturally. And excited, I thought. Anyway, he said he'd inform the rest of the members. And he left it to me to handle everything — calling the papers, getting the documents ready for display. I left and headed back to the museum."

"*Then* you changed your mind?"

"No," he said again. "Somebody changed it for me."

Mr. Bradbury reached for his paper cup. It was empty, and Katherine filled it again. He took a sip and said, "Shortly before you came back that day to find out what happened, I had a visitor. I didn't know the man, but he seemed to know all about me and our discovery."

"A reporter?" Sam asked.

"No. Not a reporter." Mr. Bradbury took a deep breath. "More like a messenger. And his message to me was to forget about making the discovery public."

Molly frowned. "Because of what you told me? That it would be bad for Lynnton?"

He almost laughed. "No, that wasn't the reason. The reason was that if I didn't, I might arrive at the museum one day and find it burned to the ground. Or, he hinted, the fire might even take place while I was in it."

Molly could only stare at him for a minute. "He really said that? That's . . ."

"A threat," Mr. Bradbury finished. "And I hate to admit it, but it frightened me. I had no idea that you were being threatened, too. But once your . . ." he glanced at Katherine. ". . . Ms. Edelman told me, I felt ashamed of myself. I wanted to explain to you, and apologize."

Molly smiled at him. "It's okay. I was scared, too." She was quiet for a second, and then she thought of something. "Wait a minute!" she said excitedly. "You said you told one man at the Lynnton Corporation. If he was the only one who knew, then he must have sent that guy to scare you off!"

"Yes, I'm sure he did," Mr. Bradbury agreed.

"Who was it?" Molly asked. "Who'd you tell?"

Before Mr. Bradbury could answer, Katherine spoke up. "It was Andrew Caleb, wasn't it?"

"The guy who owns this house?" Sam asked. "That's crazy."

"I'm afraid it's not," Mr. Bradbury said.

"Andrew Caleb," Molly said in amazement. "It was him, all along? Why?"

"You see," Mr. Bradbury said, "he never intended to build the hotel *behind* the house. He meant to tear the house down."

Molly stood up slowly, feeling like the breath had been knocked out of her. "I never thought of him, because he seemed so nice. But he was just pretending. He wouldn't want anyone to know about Sarah Woolrich. Because if they did, they'd want to see her house. It would be kind of a historical landmark. Then he couldn't tear it down and build his hotel. All he cares about is the money." Molly suddenly turned to Katherine. "How did you know?"

"I didn't know for sure," Katherine said. "I was guessing. For the reason you just said — the money. An old house and empty land don't bring in much money. But he stands to make a fortune from this hotel deal."

"He must have known the whole time," Molly said. "About Sarah Woolrich, I mean."

Katherine nodded. "His family probably passed the story along from one generation to the next, but tried to keep it a secret. Once he knew you were interested in this house, Molly, he tried to stop you — to scare you off. He sent somebody to the museum and to this house, when he knew you were alone. And he had somebody follow you and Sam on the path that day. He was trying to frighten you enough so that you'd stop looking into the history of the house."

"Yes," Mr. Bradbury agreed. "And I'm positive Andrew Caleb sent that 'messenger' to me. But I'm afraid I can't prove it."

"But wait!" Molly was excited again. She'd thought of something else. "It's not his house. Sarah wasn't *really* a witch. So Mr. Caleb's great, great . . . whatever . . . didn't have any right to it. It belonged to Rebecca. Or it should have. Not to the Calebs."

Katherine smiled. "That's exactly what I thought. Just before Mr. Bradbury got here, my office called. I asked them to find out about that for me."

"What'd they say?"

"When Mr. Woolrich died, the property went to his family, even if he didn't leave a will. And it would have been Rebecca's one day, when she was old enough. Of course, since they thought Sarah was a witch, I guess they figured the law didn't matter. But the whole idea that she was a witch is ridiculous. Some Caleb or other should have at least set the record straight after enough time had passed."

"And even though Sarah was killed," Molly

said, "the place should have gone to Rebecca."

"Yes, I think so," Katherine said. "Andrew Caleb probably knows that, too."

"No wonder he didn't want anyone to find out," Sam said. "It's not even his house! This isn't the Caleb House, it's the Woolrich House!"

Mr. Bradbury had been listening quietly. Now he cleared his throat. "Well, I, for one, don't care anymore about keeping the Calebs' secret."

Molly grinned at him. "You're going to tell, aren't you?"

"Yes, Miss Bishop." He actually grinned, too. "I'm going to tell."

"You're not scared?" Sam asked.

"Not anymore." Mr. Bradbury set his cup on the wobbly metal table. "When all this comes out, I'm sure that Andrew Caleb will have second thoughts about threatening people. I'm also sure he'll find somewhere else to build his hotel."

He walked over to the side door and then stopped. "It's interesting. After the Salem witch trials and hangings were over, the people involved realized what a terrible mistake they'd made. And most of them admitted it and tried to help the families of the victims." He sighed. "I think the least Andrew Caleb can do is give up this house for the sake of history."

"And for Rebecca," Molly said.

"Yes, I suppose you're right," he agreed with a smile. "For Rebecca. If you come back here again, Miss Bishop, I think you'll find that the name of the house has been changed. From now on, it'll be called the Woolrich House."

Mr. Bradbury shook hands with them all, even Sam. As he shook Katherine's hand, he frowned. "Ms. Edelman, I hope you don't mind my asking. But I never did get your relationship with Miss Bishop straight. You said you were her lawyer?"

Katherine laughed. "No, I said I was *a* lawyer."

"She is!" Sam said. "She really is."

"Our mother died three years ago," Molly said. "And our father married Katherine. She's a lawyer." Molly looked at Katherine, then back at Mr. Bradbury. "She's part of the family, too."

It was funny, Molly thought. In a few days, a lot of people were going to know about Sarah and Rebecca Woolrich. Mr. Bradbury said that even the newspapers in New York and other big cities would carry the story. The funny part was, they wouldn't know the *whole* story. Nobody but Molly would ever know that.

It was late now, and Molly was in bed. As usual, the room was hot. The only cool spot was where she was, right in line with the fan.

She crossed her arms behind her head and

stared at the ceiling. She wasn't sleepy at all. She felt keyed-up, almost like she was waiting for something else to happen.

All of a sudden, she knew what it was. She was waiting for Rebecca to come. This was when she'd come before, late at night.

She waited some more, listening to the fan and the crickets. But nothing happened. And then she realized that nothing more was going to happen. It was over. That sad-eyed girl with the faded dress and the heartbroken voice didn't have to come anymore. They had saved her house. And although they couldn't change what had happened to her mother, they could tell about it. Everyone would know that Sarah wasn't a witch. Her name would be cleared. And Rebecca could rest, at last.

Turning her head, Molly looked at the picture of her mother. For the first time in a long time, she didn't feel like crying. She'd always remember Ellen, she knew that. She'd probably always miss her.

But now there was Katherine. Katherine had helped her today, and somehow, things had changed. Part of the family, Molly had said to Mr. Bradbury. Once she had said it, she knew it was true.

Downstairs, the pipes gurgled and clanged. Molly smiled and waited for them to stop. When they did, the house was quiet, and it felt peaceful. Molly thought of a place at home where they could hang Katherine's painting of it — in the family room, over the fireplace. She listened to the night sounds for a little while longer. Then she closed her eyes and slept.

APPLE® PAPERBACKS

Pick an Apple and Polish Off Some Great Reading!

NEW APPLE TITLES

- ❏ MT41917-X Darci in Cabin 13 Martha Tolles $2.75
- ❏ MT42193-X Leah's Song Eth Clifford $2.50
- ❏ MT40409-1 Sixth Grade Secrets Louis Sachar $2.75
- ❏ MT41732-0 Too Many Murphys
  Colleen O'Shaughnessy McKenna $2.75

BESTSELLING APPLE TITLES

- ❏ MT42709-1 Christina's Ghost Betty Ren Wright $2.75
- ❏ MT41042-3 The Dollhouse Murders Betty Ren Wright $2.50
- ❏ MT42319-3 The Friendship Pact Susan Beth Pfeffer $2.75
- ❏ MT40755-4 Ghosts Beneath Our Feet Betty Ren Wright $2.50
- ❏ MT40605-1 Help! I'm a Prisoner in the Library
  Eth Clifford $2.50
- ❏ MT41794-0 Katie and Those Boys Martha Tolles $2.50
- ❏ MT40283-8 Me and Katie (The Pest) Ann M. Martin $2.50
- ❏ MT40565-9 Secret Agents Four Donald J. Sobol $2.50
- ❏ MT42883-7 Sixth Grade Can Really Kill You
  Barthe DeClements $2.75
- ❏ MT42882-9 Sixth Grade Sleepover Eve Bunting $2.75
- ❏ MT41118-7 Tough-Luck Karen Johanna Hurwitz $2.50
- ❏ MT42326-6 Veronica the Show-off Nancy K. Robinson $2.75
- ❏ MT42374-6 Who's Reading Darci's Diary? Martha Tolles $2.75

Available wherever you buy books...
or use the coupon below.

Scholastic Inc., P.O. Box 7502, 2932 East McCarty Street, Jefferson City, MO 65102

Please send me the books I have checked above. I am enclosing $_____ (please add $2.00 to cover shipping and handling). Send check or money order — no cash or C.O.D.'s please.

Name_____

Address_____

City _____ State/Zip _____

Please allow four to six week for delivery. Offer good in the U.S.A. only.
Sorry, mail order not available to residents of Canada. Prices subject to change.

APP589

America's Favorite Series

THE BABY-SITTERS CLUB®

by Ann M. Martin

Collect Them All!

The seven girls at Stoneybrook Middle School get into all kinds of adventures...with school, boys, and, of course, baby-sitting!